THE SERPENT WAND: A TALE OF LEY LINES, EARTH POWERS, TEMPLARS AND MYTHICAL SERPENTS

JAKE CONLEY BOOK 6

JOHN BROUGHTON

Copyright (C) 2020 by John Broughton

Layout design and Copyright (C) 2020 by Next Chapter

Published 2020 by Gumshoe – A Next Chapter Imprint

Cover art by Cover Mint

This book is a work of fiction. Names, characters, places, and incidents are the product of the author's imagination or are used fictitiously. Any resemblance to actual events, locales, or persons, living or dead, is purely coincidental.

All rights reserved. No part of this book may be reproduced or transmitted in any form or by any means, electronic or mechanical, including photocopying, recording, or by any information storage and retrieval system, without the author's permission.

Frontispiece: St Margaret and the Dragon
As imagined by Dawn Burgoyne
Medieval re-enactor/presenter specialising in period scripts. Visit her on Facebook at dawnburgoynepresents.

The Serpent Wand is dedicated to my brother-in-law, Paolo Valente

Special thanks go to my dear friend John Bentley for his steadfast and indefatigable support. His content checking and suggestions have made an invaluable contribution to
The Serpent Wand.

ONE
WARWICKSHIRE, 2022 AD

In the early phases of my psychic investigations, I received letters from trolls and cranks as well as from a few people with a genuine interest in the supernatural. Thankfully, they have become fewer as my investigative work is now largely under the aegis of HM Secret Services. However, the recent events connected with the finding of the Ely Abbey Treasure has set me under public scrutiny once more. This is reflected in the number of begging letters, cranky notes and abusive missives that now overflow from bags destined to the paper recycling plant.

Luckily, my wife, Alice, acts as my assistant and sorts the correspondence, eliminating the dross and creating a small in-tray of those worthy of attention. I trust her implicitly with this task. Occasionally it happens that I'm urged by her outraged expression to inquire about some of the worst examples and to share in her indignation, generally ridiculing the sender enough to transform her face into one of amusement.

I was settled in the brown leather swivel chair of my study sorting through the mail when I came upon a letter from Tewkesbury in Gloucestershire:

JOHN BROUGHTON

Dear Mr Conley,

I'm writing to you because — I'll spare you the tedious details and get straight to the part that caught my eye—my attention was first drawn to the line by the unusual behaviour of the birds. Geese fly along it, never deviating from place to place. At the end of the summer, swallows invariably follow the same course. Only when I studied it on an ordnance survey map, did I notice the arrow-like route passing through various sites of a particular nature. If I might be so bold, I believe there is an earth force joining them. Thus began my daily walks along the sixteen-mile route upon which I felt I was beginning to have a deeper insight into the world around me and in particular, the wildlife, the buzzards circling overhead —there followed a long series of examples of creatures of various sizes and species ending with a discourse of communing with assorted plants and even inanimate rocks. I would have dismissed the writer as simply another crank at this point, but something written below stopped me from crumpling the sheet and tossing it in the bin. Sadly, I have been forced to abandon my uplifting walks. A shadowy being began to haunt my path. At first, I put it down to my imagination but on subsequent occasions, its presence was accompanied by sensations. The hair on my arms stood up and I felt a tingling followed by an unnatural coldness given the warmth of the day. Sir, I'm convinced this entity meant me no harm but that it was not of our time. I'm not a courageous person and could not find it in me to continue my walks. I feel sure that if I had, I would have finally seen the ghost. Surely, it would have manifested itself to me as more than a shade. Your reputation as a psychic who has had dealings with the supernatural spurred me to contact you. I hope you will not consider this imp—again, I'll cut to the essence of the letter—and so, if you are interested and could spare the time, I would be honoured to invite you to a meeting in my home. Please call me on 7549 176— [I have truncated his number out of correctness] if you could see your way to obliging me.

Best regards,
Aria Gough

Alice had thought it sufficiently interesting as not to consign it straight to the bin. She'd placed it on the small to-be-read pile and I admit my interest was more than a little piqued. I'd reached a state of boredom waiting for Sir Clive Cochrane's dreaded call, made more fearful in my mind the longer it failed to come. I called through my open study window to Alice who was wielding a soapy spray, hunting spider mites among the multicoloured zinnias.

She came over and accompanied a smile with a raised eyebrow.

"This letter from Tewkesbury, what do you think of it?"

She frowned, pursed her lips and shook her head. "I'm not sure, but there's something intriguing about it and more than Mr Gooch—"

"Gough, Aria Gough. Unusual name, isn't it?"

"Yes, well, I think he's holding something back. I don't know why, call it an instinct. In any case, it looks quite your sort of thing, Jake. I know you're restless. Why don't you ring him?"

"From the letter, it sounds like a ghost is haunting his footpath and if that's true, I'm interested, all right. I'll phone him now."

Alarm bells should have started ringing the moment I discovered that Mr Gough was an intelligence researcher who commuted the ten miles along the motorway to the Doughnut— the Government Communications Headquarters in Cheltenham. With hindsight, it surprises me I didn't go straight on the defensive. I put that down to his pleasant, reliable appearance. In his early thirties, he was dressed conservatively, clean-shaven, tidy haircut and a charming smile. He surrounded himself with reassuringly normal books and boxed sets of TV series, some of which I'd enjoyed myself since I tend to binge-watch those that grab me. Physically in pretty good shape, Gough was very tall with walnut skin, grey hair and green eyes. He confessed to his love of hiking, "...which of course, is why I wrote to you, Mr Conley. If you'll allow me," he reached for a rolled-up chart and spread it across a wide tile-topped coffee table, which looked home-made, and deliberately cleared to create space for this demonstration, which was a pity for him because at that moment, his wife, Ishbel, another scientist, chirped, "Move that map, Aria, I need the table for tea and biscuits."

I was impressed that he obeyed instantly with nothing more than a loving smile and a nod. A very stable character, Mr Gough.

As soon as the ceremony was over—and I must say, I do appreciate white tea, and Ishbel's home-baked biscuits were quite delicious—he spread out the map and with some relish pointed out the route of his regular walk, which began nine miles from his home at Pershore Abbey, where he parked, then hiked passed Bredon Hill, through Beckford, Little Washbourne, which I knew as a splendid Cotswolds village, and ended at Winchcombe Abbey. My first thought was *what a coincidence* as the route started and ended with an abbey and I said so.

He looked up and smiled, "As a matter of fact, it was pure coincidence, at least, I imagine the first time I walked it, I'd had enough tramping and felt that ending there was appropriate – but with what I know now," he said mysteriously, "I'm not so sure. Look!" He moved rapidly to a cupboard and came back bearing a metre-long ruler and pencil. Laying it on the map, he joined the two abbeys and firmly pencilled a line joining them. Removing the wooden straightedge, "What do you observe, Mr Conley?"

Before I could assimilate the details, I was surprised to hear Mrs Gough, in the background, murmur, "It's all bloody nonsense!"

Either her husband didn't hear her or chose to pretend otherwise, his concentration on my face never wavered, waiting for my conclusions. They were quick in coming because his point was obvious.

"The line passes through religious sites," I tapped the first abbey, St Mary's church, Beckford, and the final abbey."

"And?" he pressed, like a schoolmaster, which irritated me.

"And...ancient monuments," my finger indicated again, "Elmley Castle, here, Bredon Hill—that's an Iron Age settlement, isn't it?—he nodded assent and I continued, "an ancient manor house here, and, finally, the Belas Knapp long barrow."

He grinned at me, his green eyes shining with enthusiasm, "And look here, just off the line, but close enough to count, is Sudeley Castle. Do you know what we've got here, Mr Conley? A ley line!"

"Piffle!" Ishbel said. The scorn she put into the one word was worth a volume. I imagined her scientific mind was far too sceptical to cope with anything even vaguely irrational. It prompted me into a reaction, "As Cardinal Newman said, *one cannot rationalise about the irrational*, Mrs Gough."

It earned me a scowl and a query, "Are you Catholic, then, Mr Conley?"

"Please call me Jake, both of you...and no, I'm not a Catholic, but the cardinal had a point. I suppose you've read about my encounter with a homicidal ghost at Elfrid's Hole?"

She frowned and tilted her head, wrinkled her nose and said, "There are some things about that I'd like to take up with you."

Her husband cut in, "Not now, darling, perhaps over dinner. You will stay for dinner, I hope Jake? Ishbel's a great cook!" He cast her a loving glance.

Since her biscuits were a recommendation, I accepted like a shot.

"I'd be delighted, thank you very much."

"Anyway," Aria said, "Back to business, as I was saying, it's a ley line, I'm sure. And my ghost proves it." He tapped his forefinger on the pencilled line at a place called Wick. I've done my homework," he smiled up at me, "there are historic sightings of the ghost of a monk here. It was a funeral path, you know, from Pershore Abbey to Wick. Jake, there's an interesting theory, and it's why I wrote to you, that there are heightened psychic activities along ley lines. You'll find sightings in several places on this one."

I have to admit, at that moment, I was so taken by the possibility of encountering ghosts that I forgot about mistrusting him, something I'd decided when I discovered his profession. Instead, I was raring to investigate the psychic phenomena along his route. Little did I realise at that cheerful moment how much the investigation would change my life and what important information he had withheld.

TWO
TEWKESBURY, GLOUCESTERSHIRE 2022 AD

Jake awoke with a sense of disorientation and it took a few seconds of staring at the elegant William Morris repro wallpaper to connect. The hospitality of the Goughs had extended beyond the excellent dinner to offering him their spare bedroom for his stay in Tewkesbury. His attempts at not imposing, brushed aside by the lure of Ishbel's cooking, had been easily overcome.

Alia Gough had timed his letter to Jake to coincide with their annual holiday and to Jake's question of why they weren't going away gave a brusque answer.

"We decided to have a complete rest at home, didn't we, darling?"

Jake, never slow to pick up on undercurrents, noted the fleeting frown, the slight hesitation and the barely detectable resentment in Ishbel's reply.

"Ah, um, yes. It's been a tough year at work and we need to unwind."

"Maybe I should find myself a hotel tomorrow, Ishbel, I don't want to be a burden."

Aria cut in with too much eagerness for my comfort, "We won't hear of any such thing. Isn't that right, darling?"

"Oh, absolutely, Jake. I have to cook for two anyway, one more portion makes very little difference. It's nice to have you with us."

But I could tell that she was being hospitable under duress. It made me feel uneasy and now, too late, began to wonder why my presence was so important to Aria Gough.

Dinner over, and questions about Elfrid's Hole answered without arousing any suspicions, over a glass of outstanding single malt, my favourite, Lagavulin—it didn't occur to me then that he was well-informed about the predilections of a total stranger—he offered to run me to Pershore Abbey in the morning.

It struck me that he didn't want me to waste any time before starting my investigations, confirmed by his attitude when I wanted to look around the surviving structure of the abbey, the next morning, and I didn't like his tone.

"That can wait, Jake, you should get straight to the path. Come this way!"

Much more of this and I'd have it out with him, but I still didn't have the full measure of the man or any inkling of what he was up to. He left me at a public footpath, signposted for Wick, and claimed that he didn't have the nerve to accompany me. We exchanged mobile numbers and he said he'd pick me up at the same spot when I was ready.

I set off along the grassy path, content to be alone but after fifty yards of feeling eyes on my back, turned to find him still there, staring at me with a curious expression on his face. The earlier unease returned and as I continued, leaving him out of sight, I tried to sort things out. When I plunge into deep thought, my surroundings, in this case, worthy of admiration, are blotted out. My steps became mechanical and I gave myself over to reflection. I ran through what I knew about my hosts and the most alarming aspect of their otherwise charming selves was that they worked for the government in a top-secret facility. This would explain how they seemed to know so much about me when I recounted the affair of Elfrid's Hole. Little signs, in hindsight, that they knew more than the general public from the news and my writings, together with knowledge of my preferences and habits, rankled.

I tramped on, oblivious to my surroundings, thinking about the tension I had picked up between husband and wife. Ishbel, careful to disguise her dissent, nonetheless, was unhappy about what was going on—whatever it was. I needed to find out fast because there was something her husband was holding back. His aggressive insistence on my current activity seemed out of character for an otherwise pleasant and easy-going personality. I decided I couldn't trust him and to find out as soon as possible whether he was acting on his initiative or whether behind his presentable front lurked some sinister figure like Sir Clive Cochrane. I shuddered and dismissed all such ideas to concentrate on my surroundings.

Hadn't Aria told me that this was once a funeral path to Wick from the abbey? I stopped, closed my eyes and dwelt on that. At last, concentrating on my present, mind open to sensations, the strong feeling of bereavement overwhelmed me as if I'd lost a loved one. For the first time in months, the familiar dull ache between my eyebrows returned until it spread to the whole of my forehead. This was a sure sign I was in the presence of psychic phenomena. I had borne this cross in the years since my road accident that had cross-wired my brain. Perhaps, after all, I would encounter the ghost Aria claimed to have sensed. I had no reason to doubt his word on that score, but I was rapidly concluding that it was only cloaking something much deeper.

Again, casting these thoughts aside, I took stock of my surroundings. The path was taking me alongside a ploughed field, and just over a slight rise, where I caught my first glimpse of the village roofs. The track led to a road, which as I followed it into the settlement, was signposted as Yock Lane. Given the rural setting, I wondered whether the name was a corruption of *yoke*. My first thought was to find a pub because by now, I was indifferent to

Gough's ghost hunt. The village was small enough for me to realise, after a few minutes, that there would be no refreshing pint of ale and on asking a local with a bushy white beard and flat cap, he indicated with his walking stick that the nearest hostelry was the Star Inn back up at Pershore.

My earlier considerations had taken away any desire to continue my hike along Aria's supposed ley line. The absence of a pub in Wick left me at something of a loose end until I saw a sign pointing to St Mary's church, which raised my spirits because one of my main hobbies is exploring ancient rural churches. The edifice didn't disappoint since I had the good fortune to find it open and occupied by a cordial sexton only too keen to explain the outstanding features of the twelfth-century building— the nave arcade and the medieval cradle roof.

"Yes," he said with pride, "the tub font was recut in the nineteenth century but it's sure to be much earlier."

Outside, I found a restored churchyard cross and looking back across the grass at the church, I admired the honey-coloured freestone walls and imagined how it might have appeared with the tower the sexton said once rose above the body of the church. Today, it was a squat building, its body articulated into three parts. The tallest feature, a square louvred bellcote perched like a chimney over the tiled roof. Not so imposing, then, as an exterior but my visit indoors had been rewarding.

In this uplifted mood, I retraced my route, this time much more aware of everything around me. The first thing I noticed was the arrow-like progress of an echelon of wild geese. Maybe there was nothing unusual about such undeviating flight and Aria had put the idea into my head, but they flew straight over Pershore Abbey. As I progressed, the earlier feeling of oppression, that sense of bereavement returned, only interrupted for a moment by the behaviour of hundreds of high-flying swifts. I know the habits of that bird well, it swoops and screeches in circles but there they were, flying straight, and that can't have been a coincidence.

When I approached Pershore, at a point three hundred yards from the end of the path, my forehead began aching and I had the sensation of being watched. My eyes searched for signs of life ahead and saw none but just as I thought there was nobody, the air seemed to move, and a dark shade slipped away before I could focus on it. This must have been the presence Aria Gough had brought me to find. I hurried up to where I had glimpsed it, apart from it being noticeably colder there, nothing was to be seen. I gathered seven pebbles and by the side of the path formed them into a letter J as a marker.

The footpath ended near a busy road, which crossed over the River Avon. I reached it once across the water, followed Bridge Street, for half a mile until I came to the Star Inn. I could put off my pint of ale no longer. A weird feeling came over me as I passed the opening in the pub wall where a sign indicated the riverside car park. I stared at this entrance for a while and decided that it was typical of an archway for coaches in bygone times. Shrugging off my negative sensations, I entered the bar. Soon it became clear that this was a historic building, a fifteenth-century coaching inn according to the owner and the exposed beams and ancient fireplace announced as much. I settled down to enjoy my beer but the verb is wrong, as all the time I sat there I was *unsettled*. My head kept turning in the direction of the archway and I couldn't help but wonder why.

It's probably for this reason that I decided against another pint despite the quality of the ale. Instead, I phoned Aria Gough and arranged for him to pick me up. Although he said he'd come at once, his tone was hostile and I couldn't think why. I was soon to find out.

"I must say, I was surprised to find you in a pub," his tone was sharp.

"Why?"

"I thought you were going to walk the whole route, so I didn't expect you back till evening." Now his voice was sulky.

"When I reached Wick, I hadn't met your ghost and frankly I was bored until I found St Mary's church. An interesting little—"

He cut me short, "I'm glad you found it. It's largely twelfth-century, you know. There's an astonishing number of churches in England dedicated to either the Virgin or Saint Michael standing on ley lines."

I ignored his manners but was developing a dislike of Mr Gough.

"You might be interested to know that, on my return, I came across your ghost." I waited for his reaction, which was immediate.

"Ah, did you? Did you get a good look at him...er...or her?"

"To be honest, I only caught a glimpse but on investigation, its presence had chilled the air. I've marked the spot and will seek it out tomorrow."

"You see, I was right. There is a ghost!"

"I think there's little doubt about it. The footpath gave me the strangest sensation."

This comment excited him so much that, distracted, he almost overshot a red traffic light.

"Did it?" His voice trembled with emotion, which seemed odd. "Did you sense some strange power?"

Now, why would he ask that? A peculiar choice of words that reinforced my growing belief that he was less interested in the ghost than in the ley line. Had the spectre been only an excuse to lure me to Pershore?

"Power? No, more a sensation of oppression, or of bereavement—but that's to be expected on the *funeral path* that you mentioned."

"Ah yes, I suppose it is," he pulled into his drive, "but no other sensations, Jake?" he insisted.

"No, none, that is if you exclude my strong desire for an ale that took me to the Star Inn."

His green eyes locked on mine and he looked grave, "Yes, that's queer, isn't it? The inn is on the ley line too and also boasts a ghost."

"Does it indeed?" My interest quickened.

"I can't remember the exact date, but the eighteenth century some time. They say a young coachman died from a fall off his horse in the archway. His ghost has been sighted on occasions."

"In the archway." I repeated.

I lapsed into silence and his pestering about sensations continued but I gave him no satisfaction and retired to my room to connect with the internet and research the area I was exploring. I had hoped to hear him drive off somewhere in my absence, so that I could catch Ishbel alone. I wanted to discover the cause of the tension between them over the matter of the ley line. But that tactic would have to wait because when I ventured downstairs, I found them chatting cosily on the lounge sofa, his arm draped around her shoulder.

"Sorry to intrude. I'll go back up."

"No-no!" they chorused.

Soon I was ensconced in a comfortable armchair with a whisky and Aria steered the conversation back to my morning hike. I was determined to keep him off the subject of ley lines and plunged eagerly into my hobby, surprising Ishbel with the depth of my knowledge about church architecture and entertaining her, more than him, with a potted gazetteer of fascinating out-of-the-way churches.

The only discordant note came over another scrumptious dinner —one of Ishbel's specialities according to Aria—a caramelized garlic, spinach and cheddar tart. Sulkily, he said,

"I think you should make a decent effort to walk the whole route."

It wasn't so much the words but the tone that irritated me.

Ishbel noticed and gave him a stern reproving glace.

"Oh, I'm sorry, I didn't mean to be insistent, but with Jake's love of churches, there's always St Mary's at Beckford near Little Washbourne. It's right on the ley line."

So, there it was, he'd resisted so far, but this remark caused Ishbel to purse her lips and avoid my gaze.

"The most important thing is to hunt down your ghost, Aria—and that's what I'll give priority to."

He looked quite peeved, "But there are many other hauntings along the ley line."

"And yet you invited me down here to sort out this particular one, didn't you? And that's what I'll do." I stared hard at him and Ishbel pushed back her chair and began to remove plates.

"Well, yes, I suppose I did. Good luck with that tomorrow then." His tone grudging, he sounded anything but convincing.

THREE

PUBLIC FOOTPATH NEAR WICK, 2022 AD

I EXPECTED TO BE UP BEFORE ARIA BECAUSE THE SUN HAD JUST nosed over the horizon but he was dressed and wide awake. That he had been waiting for me was apparent when he sprang from his armchair with,

"Ah, there you are Jake! Good morning. Up bright and early then. Coffee?"

Refreshed by the beverage, we put on our respective footwear and went out to the car.

He lost no time after bundling me into his black Audi, "I expect you'll want to hike along the ley line at least as far as St Mary's at Beckford?"

"I'll do that Aria if I don't meet your ghost before I come to Wick. Frankly, my main objective is to complete what I came here to do—to establish who is haunting the footpath. By the way, have other people reported sightings of this phantom?"

"Historically, yes. I think it has been described as a monk-like figure, which would seem right given the connection to the abbey and the funeral path."

That made sense so I pressed him. "But what about recent apparitions apart from your own?"

"Jake, I'll be honest, I didn't hang around long enough to get a good look at him. So, I can't say it was a monk or anyone else, male or female. To answer your question, I seem to remember something in the local paper a few years ago, a woman scared by a cowled figure trying to catch her attention by pointing. If I recall correctly, she said it was indicating the direction of Elmley Castle. It's another village on the ley line, by the way."

He just couldn't keep ley lines out of the conversation.

There was little traffic so early in the morning. Aria followed a white vehicle out of town to Pershore and when it parked and we passed, I saw it was a baker's van.

When my driver left me at the footpath, he noticed my gaze towards the tower of the abbey.

"Don't worry, I'll visit it after I've solved the mystery of your ghost," and with that, I set off down the path at a brisk pace. Again, I felt his eyes on my back but I refused to turn to check.

The position of my marking of a J in pebbles, anyway, was out of sight of the road. When I drew close to the marker, my skin began to feel an unnatural coldness and my forehead ached insistently until, in a second, the pain eased but the chill in the air increased. No more than five paces ahead of me stood the unmistakable figure of a monk in a brown habit, a cowl hiding his features. Not seeing his face frightened me. How was I to judge whether the apparition was a demon?

As if the ghost had interpreted my emotions, it threw back the hood and revealed a round face, which might have been pleasant except for the pallor of death. Even so, he smiled and beckoned me nearer. With trepidation, I approached, half-expecting the stench of the grave but on inspection, there was no sign of decay. As I drew near, suddenly, I heard his voice but not with my ears; instead, it resounded inside my head.

"At last, my son, my long wait is over." I noted the sigh too and the sorrow-laden tone. "It has been so long, but I knew that one day... ah well, now thou art come! O'er yonder," he pointed, as he had for the woman years ago, towards the village of Elmley Castle, "stands a water mill. There," the pointing hand trembled, "murder!"

"Murder?" I gasped.

"Ay, a drowning. The poor soul finds no rest—a mere child. Wicked betrayal in the family." The monk's emotion got the better of him and an unearthly moan made the hairs on my arm stand up. "Forgive me, son. I would not give thee cause for alarum," the gentle smile and quaintness of his archaic language calmed me. He took up his tale, as I glanced up and down the track to make sure we were alone. "Murder passed off as suicide and the victim denied a consecrated burial. Condemned by wickedness to wander this earth. It is thy bounden task, I charge thee. Go to the mill and..." The ghost faded before my eyes and beyond where he was standing, I saw a man with a black dog frisking by his side approaching.

"Mornin'," the cheerful by passer greeted me, showing no sign of disconcertion at the mysterious figure vanishing into thin air: I concluded he'd seen nothing.

"Good morning, excuse me. Am I right in thinking Elmley Castle is this way?"

"Yes, you're right. Keep along the path for four miles and you'll come to it. Lovely little village."

"Thank you. I'll be on my way. A very good day to you." The Labrador wagged its tail as if my salutation had been for her.

The ghostly monk had said enough before the interruption and I knew *my bounden task*.

Once I arrived in the village, I was cheered to see the street signs and counted four with some reference to *mill* in the name. I was also intrigued to note that the church was dedicated to St Mary— another one on this route— and hurried along to inspect it. With its crenellations, sculptures and herringbone masonry in the chancel walls, the eleventh-century building lured me inside. The interior charmed me but I'll remember my visit for the almighty ache to my forehead as I stood before the font. I admit, at that moment, I had no idea why my psychic warning was so fierce when my gaze passed over the fifteenth-century octagonal bowl and down to the much earlier square base decorated with stone-carved serpents and dragons. I do now, but I wasn't alive to the concept at the time.

Leaving the church, puzzled and restless due to that unexplained reaction, I headed to the nearby cricket field and noticed with pleasure a stream running alongside. When I reached the road at the end, I saw that it was called Mill Lane. A sharp right turn took me over grass to reach the old mill pond. I later found out that at the beginning of the twentieth century, the disused mill still stood in a dilapidated state with its thatched roof and its large wheel, as evidenced by sepia photographs made into postcards. But now there was no trace of the building. Since there was no cricket match on this weekday morning, there was nobody around as I approached the edge of the pond. I bent down and cupped my hands, raising and opening them to let the water splash back down because I didn't want to risk a bacterial infection by drinking.

As I watched, the ripples created on the placid surface fused with those in the air, familiar to my experience when episodes of retrocognition occur. The effects on my body, as always, were heavy and I was lucky not to pitch forward into the pond as dizziness overcame me. I staggered back and landed in a sitting position on the grass with a bump.

When I came to my senses, I heard a child's raised voice.

"Uncle Eli, what're ye doing? Ow! Let go, 'ee be hurting me!"

When my vision cleared, I froze in horror at what I was seeing. A heavy-set man with long, straggly hair, dressed in a fustian greatcoat was dragging a struggling boy of about seven towards the deepest water near the large slatted wheel. Now the man clamped a dirty hand over the boy's mouth so that only muffled sounds came from the pathetic writhing figure.

"It grieves me, but this is how it has to be young Master Joshua.

Thou standeth betwixt me and my inheritance. I'll not have it! Now thy father's passed away, the mill will be mine, not thine!"

The monster thrust the poor lad into the water and his anguished cry was cut short as a huge hand pushed the blond head under the water and held it there for long minutes. The merciless rogue watched the air bubbles break the surface with a hideous grin revealing a few surviving blackened teeth among the gaps. Satisfied, he released the pressure of his hand and the lifeless body of the boy floated face down, the current drifting the corpse until it rested pressed against the locked, motionless wheel. I lay low and unseen amid the grass, longer than in my century, waiting to see what the murderer would do next.

He disappeared into the mill and, after ten minutes, returned with a woman in tow.

"Ain't no accident, I'm telling thee, our Beth. The boy's been hinting at taking his life ever since our Seth died. If only thou'd heeded his words!"

"Joshua!" The woman cried when she spotted the body bobbing gently by the wheel. Her terrible sobbing and collapse into the arms of the murderer made my flesh creep. Her choked voice was hard to understand but I managed to hear.

"I never heard our Josh say any such thing, Eli."

"Nay, lass. Thou's had too much on thy mind with running the mill, and all, to pay attention to the babbling of a bairn. It's understandable, ain't it? Now, get thee off inside and I'll fish young Joshua out of the water."

I'd listened to enough of his lies and scheming, so taking a fifty pence piece out of my jeans, I stared at the head of Elizabeth II and concentrated. Immediately the air vibrated around me and when I recovered, there was no sign of the sinister figure or the mill. The grass was short and the day brighter. The sense of evil and oppression left me and I basked in the warm sunlight until, suddenly, a chill ran through my body. Looking up, I saw a blond-haired boy, barefooted and in the same clothing as the drowned child.

"Joshua!" I muttered and the boy smiled sadly, beckoning me with an impatient gesture. I stood and walked over to the ghost who turned and led me to the edge of the cricket field. There he stopped and pointed at the uneven undergrowth between two of the trees fringing the well-maintained turf of the playing area. I did not doubt that his mortal remains lay beneath the soil Picking up a small branch lying among leaf litter, I broke it in half and stuck the two pieces into the earth that the child had indicated, as a marker for my return. I turned to him,

"Don't worry, Joshua, I'll get you a place in the churchyard and I'll tell people the truth about what happened."

The boy flung open his arms for a hug and to this day, it's one of my deepest regrets. I could not find the courage to embrace a ghost. At that moment, the thought appalled me. Yet, poor creature, goodness knows how little love he'd received in his short life. The best I could manage was a quick ruffle of his blond curls— and that took some doing, believe me.

At once, I ran off without a backward glance at the child, in the direction of St Mary's. After a careful search, I discovered the vicar's phone number and that there had been a Saxon church on the site since the reign of the Mercian king, Offa. Somehow, that snippet of historical information comforted me and hinted, and there's no sense in this, that my mission would have a happy outcome.

I called the clergyman and received a polite well-measured answer. Within minutes, the Reverend Robert Lodge was beaming into my face as he shook my hand.

"It is *the* Jake Conley, the writer, isn't it? You know, I read your novel about King Aldfrith. Wonderful! Do tell me, are you writing another?"

The truth was that I had amassed a great pile of notes about my experiences in the Red Horse Vale and on Snape Common, but Sir Clive and other distractions, if you could call the Ely Treasure hunt that, had put paid to my literary dalliance. It's the sort of question that sends me 'miles away', as they say. So, I had to gather myself quickly and answer hastily, "Er, no, I've been rather busy, so the next one's on the back burner."

"Ah, I see, well more's the pity. I'll look forward to your next opus when it comes out. Now, what was it you wanted to see me about?"

I related the whole terrible story of Joshua's demise and my sighting of his ghost.

I believe the vicar was so receptive to the concept of ghosts because he had followed my career as a psychic investigator.

We were soon strolling and chatting as I led him to the unmarked grave and on the way, he confessed,

"I am most certainly of the view that unquiet spirits roam the earth seeking peace. This is especially true as in this case where a heinous crime was committed, but it also holds for example, in cases where a life has been cut short by a tragic accident."

He continued in this vein for a while until we came to the spot marked by the two twigs. He stood in silence before joining hands and reciting a prayer for the soul of the deceased. When he had finished, he turned to me,

"There's the bureaucracy, of course. We'll need the bishop's approval for exhumation and reburial. Quite honestly, under the circumstances, I can't see him refusing."

"You have my number, vicar. I'd be grateful if you'd keep me updated. If the bishop gives us the go-ahead, I'll pay for a headstone. I'm assuming there'll be parish archives with a register containing Joshua's full name and date of birth."

"Indeed, and I'd imagine the so-called suicide will be recorded too."

"And, Father, it will be my pleasure to make a substantial donation to the church funds." I went on to detail my passion for remote country churches. He was fascinated and I don't know whether it was the subject matter that intrigued him or a venial desire to assure the money I'd promised. In any case, he glanced at his watch,

"Good Lord, is that the time? Why don't you be my guest for

lunch? I don't know what Geraldine's preparing, but it's sure to be appetising, it always is."

He brushed aside my half-hearted protests, which wasn't difficult as walking makes me hungry and I also enjoy an appreciative audience for my church anecdotes. Not that there was much opportunity, as Mrs Lodge wanted all the ghastly details of the murder I'd witnessed. Luckily, she pressed me after I'd devoured her splendid steak pie or the recalled horror might have made it go to waste.

An idea occurred to me after my account of the poor boy's killing and I'm glad it did because it put my adventures in the area into a clearer context. I'll keep it to myself for now.

FOUR
TEWKESBURY, 2022 AD

Through the net curtains of the bedroom, I peered at Aria driving away unaccompanied. Not stopping to wonder where he was off to, I bounded downstairs to catch his wife alone.

"Morning, Ishbel. That's a pretty name, by the way, Scottish, isn't it?"

"Yes, my mum was a Scot, from Ayr. It means *Oath of God*."

"Does it, indeed! Does that mean you always tell the truth, Ishbel?"

She looked up from breaking an egg into a pan,

"Is there something bothering you, Jake?" I swear she had a guilty expression.

"There is. I have the distinct feeling that Aria has brought me here for reasons other than his concern about a ghost and you know what they are, don't you?"

She bit her lip and took two slices of wholemeal bread from a packet,

"Whatever you may suspect, I'm not in agreement. I told Aria to be forthright."

"What's going on, Ishbel? Is it something to do with ley lines?"

She looked startled and worried.

"I can see no harm in admitting as much but I can say no more. You'll have to ask Aria when he gets back from the supermarket— but please don't tell him I've said anything."

I smiled.

"No worries on that score. It'll come out naturally."

Her shoulders sank as her tension slipped away, "Poached egg on toast, all right?"

"Lovely, thanks."

But throughout breakfast, my mind was on Aria's mysterious behaviour and the control he exerted over his wife.

I finished eating, unrolled the ordnance survey map and studied it with a purpose. Ishbel came and went but I caught her furtive glances at me poring over the chart. By the time Aria returned carrying two bulging bags, I'd gleaned all the information from it that I needed.

"Hi, Jake, just a bit of shopping," he said pointlessly. I could see that. But I noticed his hard stare from the map to my face and back. We'd had no time so far to chat about the previous day because, having phoned my hosts to say I'd be dining out, I'd come home late and found them already retired.

He sat down and was bursting to question me but, perhaps not knowing where to start, limited himself to staring quizzically.

I put him out of his misery.

"Yesterday, I visited St Mary's and it proved interesting."

He jumped to the wrong conclusion.

"Ah, so you made it down to Beckford, at last."

"I did not."

He looked puzzled.

"Little Washbourne, then?"

"Not at all," I played him like a fish, "Another St Mary's."

He looked perplexed, frowning and chewing his lower lip. At last, he blurted, "Which St Mary's, Jake—if you're going to tell me, that is."

I was, but not yet.

"Doesn't it strike you as odd," I said, pointing to the map, "that there are so many churches with the same dedication in the area?"

He looked shifty.

"Why should it?" he said, "It's a common enough name. There must be thousands throughout the country."

"I don't doubt it, but it's peculiar that here there are four so close together in a straight line and a fifth dedicated to St Margaret if we extend it down to Alderton."

He looked more displeased than surprised or puzzled.

"What has Saint Margaret to do with this?"

"Saint Margaret is complementary to Saint Mary, just as Saint George is to Saint Michael. Legend recounts how she was swallowed by a dragon, only to kill it when she miraculously burst forth from her tragic confinement. And Saint Mary is none other than the Christianised earth goddess."

He didn't expect that and reacted sourly.

"I can see you've been doing your homework."

"Stop playing games with me, Aria. The St Mary's I visited was at Elmley Castle and at the base of the font, there are carved serpents and dragons. I've forgotten more than you'll ever know about church symbolism. For example, elsewhere in England, there are Norman representations of Saint Margaret and the dragon. The saint's head and shoulders are generally portrayed as coming out of a hole in the centre of the beast, while her heels are just disappearing into the dragon's mouth. As for St Mary's font, a churchman would cite Corinthians fifteen, verse twenty-two: *As in Adam all die, even so in Christ shall all be made alive*. But you and I know that they are there for another reason, right?

Don't pretend you don't know why! I know all about your ley line. What I *don't* know is why you are so interested in it and having me here."

Visibly relaxing, his expression returned to being as pleasant as the day we met and I like to think it showed respect for my knowledge.

"You're right and so is Ishbel. She told me to come clean with you. But look, it's better if you meet someone— my best friend, Barnes Harper. He can tell you more than me. He's also a colleague of mine."

"Is that his real name, like the bouncing bomb guy?"

I had him there for a moment, but he recovered at once.

"Barnes Wallis? The Dambusters, Operation Chastise? Er, yes, that *is* his name."

"Good, I've never met a Barnes."

When I had the pleasure, soon afterwards, Barnes Harper proved to be one of those people whose presence dominates a room, especially since, as in this case, his living room was small, and cluttered with books and charts on every available surface. He was overweight, his robust frame capped by greasy black hair. He wore light-framed rectangular glasses and had a neatly trimmed moustache and completed his persona with his garrulous, opinionated speech. Despite this, his intelligence shone through, which put me on the defensive until I knew who or what I was dealing with.

"We thought we'd get you involved, Mr Conley... may I call you Jake?"

"Please do."

"...because of your renowned psychic powers."

"What makes you think they are needed here?"

"Come, come, you must have picked up more than a hint of the power that resides in our ley line."

I looked at his wobbling chin and into the small dark eyes with barely disguised distaste, which I hoped he wouldn't notice since he was so full of his own importance. I tried a false chumminess,

"And what if I have, Barnes, surely that's not enough on its own to fetch me from my idyllic existence in Warwickshire?"

"Ahem, obviously not. But as you know, ley lines are recognised throughout the world. The Chinese call them *lung mei* or *dragon's breath* and they emit a not indifferent magnetic energy. You must have noticed the effect on the magnetite within the bodies of migratory species."

I thought of the geese and the swifts and admitted that I had noted it during my short stay.

"So, the reason we brought you here, Jake, is that we need you to determine what is going on. You will also have observed the increased psychic activity along the ley line. As you will be aware, the earth's energy can be harnessed either for good or for evil—"

Perhaps I shouldn't have interrupted at that point but I was getting impatient.

"You're right about the psychic activity. I've already encountered two ghosts. I've solved the problem of the mysterious presence for you, Aria."

Holding their rapt attention, I went on to relate the murder of the mill boy and the concern of the monk that the child should rest in consecrated ground.

"There, in a nutshell, you have the dichotomy, Jake. On the one hand, the good— the ghostly brother, with his loving intercession on behalf of the troubled soul; and the evil—the villainous murderer of his nephew and subsequent remorseless behaviour to cover the crime. We have grounds to suspect, but no more than *suspect*, that there are forces for evil trying to harness the undoubted power of the ley line. That's why we took the liberty of bringing you here."

I thought about this for a moment and didn't like it.

"If we are to proceed, Barnes, I need you both to be frank with me."

He feigned a puzzled expression, not too well, either, and I didn't miss the exchanged glances with Aria.

"What is it you wish to know, Jake?"

"I want to know who is behind your actions?"

"I'm afraid I don't understand."

"I hardly think that you two would take up some undetermined crusade against an unspecified evil and go to the trouble of involving an outsider unless you were obliged to. So, who's behind this? Sir Clive Cochrane?"

I saw at once from their confusion that this was wide of the mark.

Aria spoke for the first time, "Sir who...?"

"Never mind. Look, you both work in intelligence gathering at the Doughnut. I'm no stranger to how the Secret Service operates, meaning you can't pull the wool over my eyes."

Barnes protested, "We're not at liberty to reveal everything at this stage. You are right *and* wrong, Jake. Yes, we are acting under orders but nobody's trying to hoodwink you. Exactly the opposite, we *need* your willing cooperation."

"I see." I gazed with undisguised distaste at the portly intelligence worker. "Are you quite sure there's nothing more you wish to tell me? Something that will prevent me from packing my bags and leaving right away."

They both shook their heads, looking worried, Barnes floundered, but being the more intelligent, hit on the one thing that piqued my interest.

"There's extraordinary power in this ley. You must have noticed the number of sites." He reached for the same chart that Aria had in his lounge. "Doesn't it intrigue you, Jake? The Saxons and those before them must have known more about earth powers and how to harness them than we do. What if we could rediscover them?"

"Yes, and before they can be harnessed for evil," Aria cut in.

The unsettling, but fleeting, thought occurred to me: *How do I know that you two aren't the bad guys? You may be using me.* I would have to tread carefully, keeping an open mind. Instead, I continued to sound them out,

"Saxons, you say? But what about the prevalence of Iron Age hillforts around here? Each one associated with standing stones like Odo and Dodo, which by the way, were originally here." I pointed to the Nottingham Hill Camp, just one and a half miles north-west of Winchcombe and on the pencilled ley that Barnes had ruled down the map. Look at them all, there's the Warren Hillfort, the Roel

Camp and the Cup and Ring Stones. Apart from all of these, your ley manifests water sites and holy wells across it. They are where the underground streams break the topsoil and the pure water molecules have healing properties. Hence why they are considered holy wells, like St Kenelm's well, here," I indicated it on the map, "at Winchcombe. And then there's a spring east of Great Washbourne, here."

"Yes, yes. We now all that! A dowser can detect the magnetic stream and even the wavelengths emanating from the standing stones. Did you know that on average, it's one point eight metres from crest to crest of the waves but that can be altered by psychic activity?"

I confessed I did not.

This prompted Barnes to select three books from among the volumes scattered around the room.

"I can lend you these. I think you'd better swot up on the phenomena, Jake."

This was an excellent idea and I happily accepted the literature of an esoteric nature. Their contents didn't discourage me. Of all people, I knew that the supernatural, often invisibly, accompanies our everyday lives.

I had unfinished business in the area, especially regarding the old mill murder and, even without the pressure of these two men, would have stayed on. Now there was the added incentive of finding out what they were withholding from me and why Ishbel was so anxious. I had also developed a fascination for their ley lines that hadn't interested me until Aria Gough's letter had brought me here. In a matter of days, I had learnt much about their importance, and now I wanted to explore them in depth. This was all well and good, but I couldn't shake off the unease created by their less than open approach. Was I allowing myself to be coaxed into something dangerous, worthy of the, on this occasion, seemingly blameless Clive Cochrane?

FIVE

CENTRAL-SOUTHERN ENGLAND 2022 AD

Given my introspective nature, it was easy for me to become reclusive for three days, in which I took copious notes about the area and, more importantly, about the two earth forces that flow in something like a nervous system around the planet. Being alone and reflective is my preferred state and my hosts respected my desire for isolation. Both showed a keen interest in my progress, and what probing they indulged in came over Ishbel's splendid meals. I had the impression that their inquisitiveness came from separate directions—rather like the Michael and the Mary forces I was studying. Resounding in my mind was a quote from an old Chinese text— *The Science of Sacred Landscape*, about Feng-Shui: *There are in the earth's crust two different magnetic currents, the one male, the other female, the one positive, the other negative...* Aria questioned my progress for his, as yet unknown, purposes while she, mysteriously, seemed anxious that the said motives be somehow controlled or thwarted by my involvement.

As for me, the more I studied, the more I became convinced that I was dealing with the Mary current—the feminine earth force associated with the ancient Earth Goddess and with the waxing and waning of the moon.

I needed to investigate the Mary flow and hit on the delightful idea of combining the serious task of following the serpentine route of the Mary current with my hobby, the exploration of English churches. This would be essential because the early Church built Christian temples on pagan holy sites, which in turn were located according to a knowledge of forces largely lost to modern man. The question was where to start my quest. Where was the tail of the serpent? And did I have dowsing powers? The Mary current, differently from Michael, was associated with water sites. A careful study of the map of southern-central England took me to the River Thames. Yes, but it was a long stretch of water. I searched for the source and the nearest cartographic evidence of anything connected with St Mary. This brought me to place called Castle Eaton, over the border in Wiltshire, whose parish church was dedicated to St Mary the Virgin.

I worked steadily on planning an approximate route, subject to change, which might depend on what I discovered once on the ground. It became clear even at this stage that I required time and energy to make my way from the serpent's tail to its head.

"Aria," I said, "I'm away for at least a week. If I'm ever to understand your ley line, I should trace it from its origin."

I had no idea how he would react because I'd considered a range of ideas about my host from the most positive to things that didn't bear thinking about. So, I was surprised at his affable reaction.

"You see," I continued, "Barnes's books have been a revelation to me and if I'm to understand the forces we're dealing with, I'll have to do that on the ground."

"Of course." He looked pleased.

"But it's going to take time to establish the route and a deep examination of the nature of the ley. I have some notions but need to verify them. When I get back, I'll expect some answers, Aria, and I mean, I want the whole truth," I turned my head to smile at his wife, "and from you too, Ishbel."

She darted a frightened glance at her husband, whose almost imperceptible nod didn't escape my sharp eye.

He took a deep breath and said,

"Is there any reason why I shouldn't accompany you on this *quest?*"

"Several reasons, but the most important is that I'll want no distractions. No, I must do this alone, I'm sorry. But you can drive me down to Castle Eaton if it's no problem."

"Of course, but I'll have to look it up on the map and type it into the sat-nav. We'll give you your answers when you return. I apologise for keeping you in the dark."

He was being almost too cordial to be true, I thought and it put me on the defensive.

"Good, I'll grab my backpack and a few things and we can set off."

On departure, neither of us noticed an insignificant grey Nissan pull out after us and follow us at every turn to our destination. Why would we? On the journey through the tedious traffic, Aria did his best to pump me for information, perhaps probing to ascertain the extent of my knowledge. I fed him a few inconsequential titbits just to make conversation but didn't let him glimpse the true areas of my concern.

The pleasant village of Castle Eaton vaunted a signposted lane that led to a lynch gate into the churchyard. For reasons of my own, I refused to walk it until I was sure that Aria had driven away. I didn't notice the Nissan parked across the road even then. Only when I was sure Aria had gone did I overcome my worry that I might need to obtain a dowsing rod. Not at all, by emptying my mind, concentrating on underground water, to my delight and surprise, I detected the quicksilver flow as a silver ribbon just like an experienced dowser might have done. The first thing that struck me, as I turned on my heel, was that my preconceptions were wrong. The Mary current was neither narrow nor straight. At least ten yards wide, it made a dramatic sinuous curve towards the lane I was about to walk down. My concentration was so fierce that a bearded man wearing a flat cap and getting out of the grey car didn't register in my consciousness. Lost to my surroundings, mind fixed on the silver flow, I noted almost subconsciously that the path ran along between grass verges flanked by stone walls, the higher to my left, the lower on my other hand. The lane, shaded by tall trees, their leaves dappling my progress with broken patches of sunlight, led direct to a wooden lynch gate. I let myself through and, expecting the Mary current to run straight to the church, was amazed when it swept to my right and headed to a corner of the churchyard. I followed, intrigued, to arrive near the ivy-clad wall where stood an ancient shaft on a large rectangular plinth. The cross on top had long gone and the shaft, plain and undecorated, was perhaps half its original height. When I turned around, my eye passed unseeing over the wiry man taking a photograph towards me across the churchyard.

The meaning of this phenomenon was unclear until I touched the smooth stone and felt the earth power surge up it and reinvigorate me, removing my tiredness, filling me with an acute awareness of the beauty of my surroundings and a sense of wellbeing. Reluctantly, I removed my palms and glancing at the foot of the monument, saw that the current was only now heading for the church. It ran unswerving to the wall of St Mary's and entered the building, as I also hoped to do, not least to pick up the trail of the serpent.

I was disappointed to find the building locked but easily picked up the flow on the north side of the building. It flowed inconveniently for me through the boundary wall and continued northwards. Like a furtive schoolboy, I climbed over in pursuit. Luckily, there was nobody around to observe my inelegant scrambling—or so I thought. Back outside the church grounds, I let my concentration lapse for a moment and the virtual silver line vanished from my mind. Taking the ordnance survey map of the area from a side pocket of my rucksack, I turned it in my hand until I was able to determine where the northward direction led. Given my acquired knowledge from Barnes's books that the Mary current is associated with water, it came as no surprise that the Thames meandered little more than fifty yards to the north. I concentrated on the silver ribbon again and traced it right to the river, where it followed the water course. According to my chart, it was headed towards the village of Kempsford. A thrill ran through me because this was the line I had predetermined without the benefit of confirmation from the Mary flow itself. I had opted for this settlement simply because its church was dedicated to Saint Mary.

My reading had revealed that the Battle of Kempsford occurred on 16 January 800 AD when Aethelmund led a group of Hwiccians from Mercia in a raid against the Wiltsaetas people of Wessex. However, Weoxtan set the Wiltsaetas on them, driving them back across the river. In the slaughter, both leaders were slain—my other love was Anglo-Saxon history.

At a certain point, the Mary serpent writhed into the water and, I had to assume, crossed it. Gazing at my map in desperation I realised that I'd have to cross the Castle Eaton road bridge carrying a lane between Cricklade, four miles to the southwest, and Kempsford one and a half miles to the east. With a shrug of resignation, I recognised that there would be much backtracking and detouring to follow the subterranean current across England, and here, the Thames was a natural barrier. My heart sank at the thought of the man-made ones that might face me as my quest unfolded. I lost an hour but later picked up the Mary line as it emerged on the northern bank and writhed on towards St Mary's church in Kempsford. Unknown to me, from the bridge, a bearded man with a flat cap was watching me through binoculars.

The church was open and the Mary current ran straight through the altar and out the rear of the building. I shall not describe every church I visited in detail, except to refer to the power of the force. Apart from the dedication of the edifice, here there was nothing for me. A niche, sadly empty, lacked the statue where Mary once stood. I filled a page of my notebook, indulging my passion for churches and will share one gem that I found: in the mid-fourteenth century the heir to the earldom of Lancaster, a young boy named Henry, drowned in the river at Kempsford in a tragic accident. His father, the Earl, decided to soothe his grief by joining the war with France. As he rode away from Kempsford his horse cast a shoe. The villagers nailed the horseshoe to the church door, and there it has stayed ever since.

Happy and uplifted after my visit, glancing at my watch, I promised myself lunch at the next place Mary took me. As it turned out, I didn't have far to hike because the silver stream led me straight to Fairford, which again is by a river, this time, the Coln. It also contained a fine coaching inn, the Bull Hotel, which served hot meals and there I rested and had lunch before my visit to St Mary's church. There was no coincidence in the dedication, I reflected as I ate my meat. Most of these churches were Norman, constructed on previous Saxon sites, which in turn, were built on pagan temples. The Normans, with experience of the Near East, particularly the Templars who had a profound knowledge of earth forces, applied their esoteric learning to construction that would benefit from the benign underground power emanating. People at other tables were enjoying their food and there were enough of them to conceal the presence of my bearded shadow.

My next stopping place, St Mary's, Fairford was a delight to me because it contained twenty-eight of some of the best-preserved medieval stained-glass windows in the country. It was worth the visit to this church, rebuilt in the fifteenth century for the Great West Window alone, with its Last Judgment, but there was nothing to help me with my quest. Except to say that remarkably, once more, the Mary force passed right through the altar.

Inspection over, I set off again wherever she would lead me, which proved to be a place with a close affinity to the Virgin. The church of Meysey Hampton was dedicated to Her but did not offer me any insights, so I pressed on to the next meander of the silver thread to a place where the village name, Ampney St Mary, was taken from the Ampney brook and the church. My legs were beginning to ache from hiking, but my eyes were enraptured by the verdant countryside, alive with birdsong. Here, it was not nature that enthralled me, but a mason's carvings of two serpents on the north nave doorway. This is what I had come so far to see. This St Mary's fitted my theory to perfection. Here were the two serpents, representing the two earth forces and close by, the brook, let alone the dedication of the building. The spirit of the place, I sensed, was strong, and the line passed through the tower which marks the spot as being special. It affected me, imbuing strength as well as spirit. I didn't know how much I'd need those qualities as I noted a bearded man with a flat hat pulled down over his brow, binoculars around his neck, scribbling into a small notebook. It seemed I wasn't the only person interested in the carvings.

Apart from the brook, my chart showed the area to be full of varied water features—reservoirs, streams, canals, and springs, but to my disappointment, I couldn't find a holy well nearby. The afternoon was wearing on and I needed to think about overnight accommodation and a chance to reflect on my findings. I couldn't shake off my despondency, but looking back, I realise that my expectations of Ampney St Mary were too high and fired by my initial enthusiasm for the quest. I wanted to feel then that the serpentine line had brought me to a place attuned to lunar-type influences, with its associated healing, prophecy, visionary trances and psychic relations with elemental energies. But this was me deluding myself with wish fulfilment.

Later, I was to find more powerful nodes, but at that moment, I trudged on following the current to a place called Bibury—one the nineteenth-century pre-Raphaelite artist, William Morris, described as *the most beautiful village in England*. The sight of it, at the end of a long tiring, but rewarding, day's hike, with its lovely Cotswold stone cottages and, best of all, the fifteenth-century Catherine Wheel pub with many exposed original ship's timber beams, prints and photographs of Old Bibury, revived me. There, I slaked my thirst with more than one fine ale. Startled, I recognised a fellow drinker with his beard and binoculars. I gave him a smile and a friendly nod, but he looked away shiftily. His reaction bothered me slightly. Was he following me? Or was I being paranoid? Why would anyone follow me around old churches? I would find out why much later. For the present, I found another hotel, the Swan, a former coaching inn by a bridge and the babbling River Coln, that offered bed and breakfast. By now, relieved to have ended my day's research, I no longer noted the presence of water and another St Mary's church nor the bearded man photographing me entering—I just wanted to rest and think.

SIX

COTSWOLDS INTO WORCESTERSHIRE 2022 AD

Across the river, standing in deep shadow, unknown to me, the bearded man trained his binoculars on the entrance of the Swan Hotel and waited patiently. At last, not that I'm a late riser, I emerged and shrugging a rucksack on my shoulders, consulted a map and turning left strode down the main road. Although I had no idea, my pursuer hurried across the bridge and followed at such a discreet distance that I failed to spot him. This came to my knowledge within days.

St Mary's, Bibury, as I might have expected, stood a hundred yards from the River Coln and the silver thread in my mind flowed right along the church and through the altar. But apart from some interesting historical snippets, there was nothing else in stone to suggest the ley line. Instead, on the south wall at the back of the nave hung a large framed eighteenth-century Italian embroidery. It depicted Saint Margaret of Antioch killing the dragon that tried to swallow her. I assumed from this that, even as late as the 1700s, people were aware of the serpentine force running through the building. Interestingly, there was once an uncovered well in the churchyard of a neighbouring church at Bisley and, in the thirteenth century, the priest fell into it and drowned. Angered by the accident, the pope placed Bisley under interdict so that Bibury graveyard had to host the dead in the so-called *Bisley piece*. This intrigued me and reminded me of the association of wells with the Mary earth force.

A seven-mile winding ramble, unexpectedly south-westwards, took me past Ampney Knowle and into the town of Cirencester, where apart from a series of St Mary's churches firmly on the ley line and surprising for their number, I had nothing to note except the incessant traffic and its tiring noise. After lunch in Cirencester, I hiked the fourteen miles north-west to Painswick, a small village near Stroud. By this time, I was too tired to visit the church and found a bed and breakfast for the night. I was still oblivious to the man dogging my tracks, but he'd arrived all right.

I had to think deeply about what was happening because, consulting my map, I failed to see how the ley line might connect from here to my proposed arrival point at Pershore Abbey. I seemed to be right off course, but I wasn't allowing, at that moment, for the serpentine nature of the Mary current.

Somewhat dismayed, the next morning, I visited the uninspiring church of St Mary, Painswick. Its churchyard was more impressive than the building with magnificent eighteenth-century headstones and ninety-nine yews. I reckoned that the local legend of the hundredth yew was fanciful nonsense. They claimed that there were ninety-nine because the hundredth planted always died. Still, tasty morsels like this, and my long-established interest in country churches, kept me going along, what seemed then, the disheartening ley line.

It took me from there to the city of Gloucester, which I knew from previous visits to its wonderful cathedral. But I was in no mood for sightseeing as the combination of concentrating on the silver ribbon and the dangerous roads of zooming traffic to cross was hard to cope with. Only the number of churches dedicated to the Virgin in and around the city surprised me—each without exception on the ley line. My dismal mood at not having my theories confirmed was enlivened by the church of St Mary de Crypt, where I discovered buried there, Jem Wood, a banker and miser, who was the model for Scrooge in the Charles Dickens novel *A Christmas Carol*.

When I arrived on the outskirts of the city at St Mary the Virgin at Rudford, I felt like giving up my quest. True, the ley line ran through the church and it was situated close to the River Leadon, but there was nothing else for me there except a pub. Luckily, things were about to change. In any case, I find that a good pint of ale puts a rosier complexion on things.

Enjoyment of my hobby isn't the point, but Cheltenham minster, dedicated to St Mary, uplifted me and not only for its splendid stained-glass rose window. It stands by the River Chelt, of course, on an eighth-century Saxon site. There's no evidence of that in the twelfth-century structure but personal preferences left behind, I swallowed my disappointment and followed the flow, which brought me to the Pitville Pump Room. There, in 1716, a mineral spring was found and exploited, resulting in them affixing Spa to the name of the town. Here, the sensation of well-being provided by the overwhelming Mary force reinvigorated my tired body after its eleven-mile hike following lunch, but it also made my head spin because of its strength. Still, I hadn't awakened to its power.

I stopped concentrating on the ley line for the day and found suitable accommodation, never suspecting that I was still being shadowed. My negative thoughts were directed towards the Doughnut, the Government Communications Headquarters (GCHQ), the British cryptography and intelligence agency in this town. I could hardly believe that I was tramping around the countryside following magnetic earth currents thanks to two of its employees. Their connection with espionage unsettled me and made me wonder what exactly underlay this curious quest. I couldn't deny the presence and power of the ley line. But I questioned the point of my tracing its course. I still hadn't realised the possible implications for the powers I possessed or even begun to suspect far worse consequences.

Fortunately, the next day restored my faith in the venture since the ley line wound on—encouragingly northwards towards my destination— to a place called Bishops Cleeve. But there I learnt something more with the finding of my first node, the point where the Michael current intersects with the Mary ley, in this case, inside the nave of the church.

My interest was aroused by St Michael's beautiful Norman doorway, with typical chevron carvings above the crenellated arch. Around the outside, and my heartbeat raced, were two dragons with intertwined tails each swallowing another creature. What could be a clearer sign of the Michael and Mary forces acting together?

Concentrating on the silver ribbons, I emerged from the delightful interior and rounded the building, in time to see a bearded figure dodge behind a clump of trees in blossom.

"Hey!" I yelled, to no avail.

Their slender trunks allowed me to see him scramble over the stone perimeter wall and I could just see his flat cap as he hastened away. There was no question in my mind that this was the same person I'd seen twice before. There could be no doubt that he was following me and taking notes about my visits, but why?

Leaving the Michael ley behind as Mary separated and, to my relief, headed north-east after flowing two hundred yards together with the masculine current. I walked past a parked grey car with two men inside, not noticing them in particular and followed the winding silver line up a public footpath running beside a field. I hiked across country as midday came and went until after six miles, I came to the village of Winchcombe, which I remembered was the end of Aria Gough's sixteen-mile ley line. I wondered if he had any idea that it snaked down to Castle Eaton on the Thames where my long hike had begun.

Winchcombe has a timeless quality, where Cotswold stone cottages are enhanced by black and white half-timbered buildings, narrow side streets and charming houses, making for a lovely village.

I'm not sure whether I was disappointed when the silver ribbon ran past ignoring the delightful parish church of St Peter's, following instead, the course of the River Isbourne, before veering sharply eastward into open farmland. I was puzzled, wondering where it was bound until, after a muddy tramp across squelchy grassland, I came to a neat man-made structure. This hidden treasure hadn't been mentioned in the books I'd studied. My map bore the gothic wording **St Kenhelm's Well**. The Mary current had brought me to a holy well!

The construction of the well-head was plain, with a tiled roof, gables at each end, and eaves decorated with a simple dentil pattern. The walls are of large limestone blocks, and the only decoration is at the entrance end. A pair of chamfered windows flanked a niche containing a carving of St Kenhelm beneath a pediment. Kenhelm was seated, carrying a sword in his right hand and an orb in his left. Above his head is the date AD 819 and below his feet the Latin version of his name, *St Kenulmus*.

I found a guide book later that informed me that there had been a sixteenth-century chapel by the well, with a well-head beside it, but the edifice was torn down in 1830. In 1887 the owner of nearby Sudeley Castle had the well-head rebuilt in honour of Queen Victoria's Golden Jubilee. The new construction reused stones from the previous chapel building. But what interested me, then, was the strength of the Mary power as it surged around the well.

Had I known what it could do for me, I'd have acted differently. Instead, I promised myself I'd find out about this saint when I had the chance. I'll recount his fantastic story elsewhere for I must move on with this account, as I did from the well, as Mary doubled back before sweeping off northwards again. I needed a rest and food after hiking twelve miles that long morning. The lengthening shadows and my watch confirmed that I should have paused at least two hours earlier. Would the Mary current take me to a place where I could refresh myself or would I have to lie down in the shelter of a wall in the open countryside?

As luck would have it, the silver flow conducted me along the

Gretton Road, where after a while, on the right, I spied the Royal Oak public house. Never was a sight so welcome. Owing to the late hour, the kitchen was closed but I managed to order a ploughman's lunch and a refreshing pint of beer.

When I'd rested sufficiently, I set off with renewed enthusiasm because before leaving the Goughs' I'd read about Becca's Ford crossing the Carrant Brook in Saxon times. Modern Beckford takes its name from the ford. I'd also learnt that back then, there had been an eighth-century minster, which had disappeared without a trace. Perhaps that was the spot where my Mary force became particularly strong for no apparent reason near the brook. The village was full of springs and the Romans had settled in this valley at the foot of Bredon Hill in 70AD. The nearby Fosse Way is a lasting reminder of their presence.

In my tired state, the last thing I needed was for the Mary line to deviate and head off up Bredon Hill, but this is what it did. Aria Gough had made no mention of his ley writhing uphill and down dale, damn him! On the one hand, my body ached; on the other, it was too early in the day to settle down for the night. I figured there was still three hours to dusk and remembered reading about the hill having an Iron Age hillfort known as *Kemerton Camp*, abandoned in the first century AD after a ferocious battle. With renewed keenness, I let the silver ribbon lead me up there past the distinguishable earthworks to the top of Bredon Hill, where Parsons Folly stood and the inner rampart ran. Was there something John Parsons MP knew about earth forces in the mid-eighteenth century when he had his summer house erected there? It seemed too much of a coincidence that the force was swirling so powerfully around it. I couldn't believe he built it just for the spectacular view.

What happened next opened my eyes to the power of the Mary flow I'd been following across England. It swept away down to a standing stone. From my research and from a trick of the low sunlight that modelled its craggy features, I knew that this was what the locals called *the Elephant Stone* and it, indeed, in that light startlingly resembled that creature. Its real name was the *Banbury Stone*, deriving from *Baenintesburg*, the name of the fort in the eighth century.

I sauntered up to it feeling quite devoid of energy, drained, that is, until I rested my palms flat on the rough stone, where my silver ribbon, running straight to it, amazingly reared up and circled it in a spiral. My hands and arms tingled but I could feel myself becoming one with the rock as if I were absorbing it spiritually...or it absorbing me. Whichever it was, I was suddenly full of energy and strength, my earlier weariness shrugged off.

"Well, well, what have we here? You just have to keep poking in your nose, don't you?"

There he was, the bearded fellow with a flat cap and a gun in his hand pointing straight at my chest.

"Like to tell me what you're doing up here fondling that stone?"

"Yes," I said, "recharging my batteries. You should try it. The rock can give you energy and wellbeing."

To this day, I don't know why I said those words to a man threatening me with a gun, but there it is.

"I might just do that," he said, pushing the weapon into his belt, stretching out his arms, palms upwards and pressing against the stone. I'm still not sure what happened then but I'll try to put it into words. A cry ripped from his throat as he was flung backwards in an arc as if a mighty electric shock had blasted through him. He fell and struck his head on a half-buried rock emerging from the turf. My first thought was that he was dead but on closer inspection, I discovered a weak pulse. What had happened? It had occurred so fast that I'd not found out who he was or why he had pointed the gun at me. What was I going to do? Up here, isolated, far from help. Well, the first thing was to relieve him of his pistol and to set his cap aright, which had shifted to cover his eyes and nose.

I went back to the stone, and touched it gingerly, more than a little afraid that it would repel me too. No such thing. I think it was touching the stone that provided inspiration. I remembered suddenly that over the brow of the hill were two other standing stones smaller than the Banbury Stone. They were known as the King and Queen and local legend maintained that anyone passing between them would be cured of illness. It was a slim chance but after what I'd just witnessed anything seemed possible. Also, a similar blow to the head might produce internal bleeding and death. Even if he had pointed a gun at me, I didn't want him to die. Dead men answer no questions.

Grasping his ankles, I blessed fate that I was dragging him downhill and not up. He was senseless and, therefore, heavy, but I made it between the stones and only then sensed the Mary current swirling around them. The unconscious man began to groan and his eyelids to flicker. I pointed his gun at him as a precaution and watched anxiously to be sure the cure was working. There seemed little doubt of that when he sat up shakily and said,

"What happened to me, up there?"

"Never mind that. Be warned, I know how to use this thing and I've killed in the past."

Neither was true, but he wasn't to know that. "I want some answers from you, smart-ish or it's curtains for you."—I remembered those words from a gangster film.

"What's your name and why have you been following me?"

He stared at me and I could see him weighing up his chances of rushing me to seize the gun.

"Don't try anything stupid and no harm will come to you. Answer my questions!"

"My name's Luke Farthing and the Brotherhood tasked me to follow you. A right merry dance you've led me across half of England, too."

"The Brotherhood?"

"Yeah," his eyes narrowed and he looked sly, "here, you know nought about us, do you?"

"I don't, I'm just enjoying my hobby of visiting churches and monuments."

"Don't give me that! You're working for the government! We

know all about you—a darned sight more than you do about us, it seems. Hasn't that bastard Gough told you?"

"He's told me nothing. What Brotherhood?"

"The Brotherhood of the Wand—and that, mate, is all you'll get out of me. Take my advice, pack your bags and clear off to wherever you came from and leave Gough and his cronies to tidy up their mess."

I pointed the gun at the man.

"Here, steady on mate! I can't tell you any more, honest. It's more than my life's worth."

I had no intention of shooting him but I needed to know why they'd sent him after me. Pausing for thought, I hesitated. On reflection, I decided that it was Aria who owed me explanations. I was more likely to find out about this Wand organisation from him or Barnes than from this cowering wretch.

"I'm not going to hurt you because I believe you're just a pawn in someone's game. Don't even think about following me anymore or I *will* shoot to kill!"

With that, I walked away down the hill. I'd done more than enough for one day. The gun was handy insurance and once checked that he hadn't stood up, and being well down the hillside, I slipped it out of sight in a side pocket of my rucksack.

By the time I arrived on the road, I'd come to a decision—a matter of priorities. The rest of the Mary ley line to Pershore could wait. My interrogation of Aria could not, so I took out my mobile and told him to pick me up as soon as possible in Beckford.

Mr Aria Gough had a lot of explaining to do.

SEVEN

TEWKESBURY 2022 AD

The comfortable seat of Aria's Audi and my weariness denied each of us the eagerly-sought answers we awaited.

"Wake up, old man!"

The gentle, insistent shaking of my shoulder brought me out of deep fatigue-induced sleep. My bleary ones looked into his amused green eyes.

"My word, you must have been exhausted, you've been snoring all the way here. But we're back and I can get Ishbel to prepare you something—"

"No, please, all I need is a bed. We'll catch up in the morning," I said, as I forced my aching frame out of the car.

The next morning, I lay thinking before getting up, my mind churning over what I planned to ask my host and deciding how much, in turn, I intended to share my findings.

A refreshing shower and hearty breakfast completed, over which I informed Ishbel of the many miles I'd hiked during the days I'd been away. I recounted to her a couple of the more interesting historical snippets I'd picked up from my church visits but told her little of importance.

Aria came in from the garden.

"Ah! You're up and about, Jake. Have a good night's sleep?"

We exchanged pleasantries before deciding to sit in the lounge and move on to more important matters. Ishbel excused herself with a list of household tasks to be dealt with.

He began, "So, did you find anything of interest between Castle Eaton and Beckford?"

"A great deal but I won't enlighten you, my dear Gough, not until you come clean."

A raised eyebrow was all he managed, so either he was a consummate actor or he had nothing to hide. I would decide which.

"Come clean? Well, yes, I suppose you're right to put it like that. I don't much appreciate subterfuge myself, but as Barnes said, we were acting under orders. We nee—"

"Whose orders?"

"I'm coming to that. Have you heard of the Aetherius Society, Jake?"

The name was new to me and I shook my head.

"Barnes and I are members of the local branch. It's an organisation founded by Dr George King back in 1955. The greatest ever spiritual guide," his eyes shone with a fanatical light I had never before seen in their green intensity, "May I quote him?"

"Please do."

"*Spiritual energy, when it is used by people, is the key which will unlock all the doors to all problems ever facing mankind.*" He sighed and looked at me, searching for understanding and approval.

"Is your Aetherius Society a religious organisation, then?"

"Good heavens, no. It transcends religion and even this planet."

"Not some kind of cranky New Age philosophy, I hope."

"Some might say that but I'd deny it wholeheartedly. Anyway, we were instructed, Barnes and I, to bring you gradually into our midst because of your extraordinary gifts, which—"

I'd had enough of this nonsense for the moment and cut in.

"Who is Luke Farthing?"

For the first time that morning, his expression became shifty."

"Luke...who?"

I didn't believe him.

"It looks like the end of the road, then, Aria. I warned you that I'd pack my belongings and leave if you were less than frank with me."

I stood up and headed for the lounge door.

"Don't go, Jake. I beg you to understand that I need authorization on this." He waved his mobile at me.

"I'm going to fetch down my bags. You make your call and tell whoever it is that if I don't receive honest answers, they can forget about Jake Conley."

I came down with my rucksack and a small holdall, dumping both ostentatiously on the carpet.

"Well?"

He cleared his throat and tried on a charming smile.

"Please sit down. I have total clearance but will require assurances that you'll keep our conversation strictly private."

Seeing no cause for objection, I nodded and muttered, "Go on."

"Luke Farthing is a member of the Brotherhood of the Wand."

"Ah, he told me as much."

"Did he indeed? What else did he say, Jake?"

"Not a lot, because I had to relieve him of his gun and then restore him to consciousness."

He stared at me slack-jawed, "You overcame and disarmed Luke Farthing!" His tone was one of extreme respect."

"In a manner of speaking." I unbuckled the side pocket of my backpack and laid the weapon on the coffee table. "Tell me about this Brotherhood."

Round-eyed, he gazed speechless at the gun, swallowed hard and cleared his throat.

"As you've gathered, they're dangerous and our sworn enemies. Where did you run into Farthing?"

"You forget, Aria. *I'm* asking the questions until I'm satisfied. Tell me about the Brotherhood."

Lips pressed tight, he still hadn't detached his gaze from the gun, but said,

"Typical, isn't it, that a society dedicated to evil should appropriate to themselves a symbol for good. You'll remember the wand of Hermes and that of his son Asclepius, through the possession of which a man becomes the master of healing?"

My interest was aroused now because of the two serpents.

"Of course, the wand topped by a sun disc with two snakes entwined around it—the sign you can see over many a chemist's door."

"Bravo! But this Brotherhood isn't devoted to healing. They are more interested in the two serpents."

"The Mary and the Michael forces?"

That shook him to the core and he could only gape, I almost heard his thoughts whirring.

"You know more than I thought."

"Never mind that. Answer my question."

He puffed out his cheeks and let the breath out slowly.

"It's knowing where to start…apart from one or two, like Farthing, who does their dirty work, their members are closeted in deep secrecy. They practise the black arts and number some of the richest and most powerful people in the land. Black magicians want to rule us, use us and divert us from the righteous path." His tone grew bitter, "Their goal is to try to eliminate spirituality because true soulfulness gives power to each individual. For them, no holds are barred, and if necessary, they will kill anyone who stands in their way. If they fail to destroy the great masters or their followers, they then infiltrate these spiritual groups, so that later on they can dominate them. This is how organized religion is created and they've tried with us but without success." An outraged glance seemed to measure whether he'd gained my support.

I couldn't honestly say because, by nature, I was distrustful of organisations. I was too much of a loner to enrol in anything that required membership. Aria Gough would have a lot of persuading to do to involve me in the Aetherius Society.

"So, why is Ishbel so anxious and at loggerheads with you?"

He glanced at the kitchen door, but it was firmly shut and the sound of a washing machine going through its spin cycle reassured him.

"Can't you guess? She believes her Head of Department is a member of the Brotherhood. And whilst they know Barnes belongs to the Aetherius Society and they keep a watch on him, they think we are just good friends and colleagues. That's why Ishbel wants me to stop associating with Barnes and why she didn't approve of involving you in what she thinks is esoteric nonsense."

"But it isn't, is it?"

"What, sorry?"

"Ley lines and standing stones. They aren't just esoteric gibberish. They are places of power."

Aria leapt out of his seat and grabbed my hand.

"So, you *do* understand! And you are...with us?"

Halfway, he changed the statement into a question.

"That depends, Mr Gough. I haven't asked all my questions yet."

"Ask away, then."

"I want to know everything you've discovered about earth energies. All of it, mind!"

He sat again slowly, never taking his eyes off my face.

"There's a lot to tell and much of it outside my competence. Would you object if I brought Barnes here to explain?"

"Will that be safe? I mean, now they know I'm involved in your activities. If they had any doubts, what happened on Bredon Hill will dispel them."

"Luke Farthing? He won't dare do anything in this residential area—and you have to realise, Jake, that the last thing the Brotherhood wants is to be in the public eye."

"Call him then."

When the doorbell rang, Ishbel opened the door and I heard her gasp from the hall and cry,

"Barnes! What's happened?"

He hobbled into the room with a black eye, a swollen and split lip with dried blood over the cut, arm in a sling and a noticeable limp. It seemed every step was painful.

Aria repeated his wife's question, his expression appalled.

"The Brotherhood," he said with difficulty, I barely understood his distorted speech and dare say, wouldn't have if we hadn't just been talking about that organisation, "I've been warned," he managed, but Ill not be scared off."

I had to admire his fortitude and slipped the gun back into my rucksack with the thought that I might be needing it.

Aria and I pressed Barnes for the details of his assailants but they'd jumped him, covered his head with a black cloth hood and he hadn't seen them. All he recalled was a gruff voice mercifully calling off the bully boys, who had been kicking him as he lay on the floor of his lounge. I thought it a miracle that there'd been room for an attack in that restricted space.

"Yeah, his voice was gravelly, but he was well-spoken, educated, not some yob off the street."

"And that's all you can tell us?" I asked.

"They said the Brotherhood of the Wand wouldn't tolerate any more interference and they mentioned your name."

"Did they?"

"They said you'd better get off back to where you came from. And to tell you, you were risking your job at Whitehall."

At this stage, he asked or a glass of water and while he sipped it, I considered the implications of his last statement. It meant someone in the Brotherhood, someone with influence had strong contacts with MI5 and knew about my work for them. Of course, the Doughnut! Well, an hour ago, I might have upped and taken my bags but not now. Barnes and Aria were treading on someone's toes. And that someone was threatening me now. Whilst I resented that, and I'm not the hero some would paint me, now I was vexed and too interested in the earth forces I'd discovered, and wanted to find out more.

Barnes was clearly in a much more comfortable state than when he'd arrived. Even so, I asked him,

"Do you feel up to explaining everything you can to me about the Mary current hereabouts?"

To my relief, he nodded and gathered his thoughts.

A hard stare to quell my scepticism preceded his argument,

"I'm not about to blitz you with mumbo-jumbo or cranky ideas, Mr Conley. I'm talking scientifically here. The scientific investigation of energy effects at megaliths dates from 1977 when Dr Eduardo Balanovski took geomagnetic measurements at a standing stone. In that year, it was decided to proceed with a two-pronged approach: a physical one, measuring known energies and a psychic archaeology programme using dowsers and psychics on site." Pausing for effect, he reproduced the same fixed look and a smile twitched at the side of his swollen lip under the bristling moustache. Another sip of water and, satisfied he'd hooked a big one, he continued, "All sorts of technology was brought into play, like a wide-band ultrasonic receiver of the 'bat-detector' type. Invariably, megalithic sites are located close to geological faults where there are localised regions of disturbed electromagnetic energy. Strange to say, there are consistent historical reports in these places of unusual light phenomena. Sorry, am I boring you?"

"Not in the least, I was trying to remember something about Cornish miners in one of your books."

"You're right. In the nineteenth century, tin miners returning from work claimed to have seen 'lights burning and fairies dancing on and around the Carn Gluze round barrow on the coast at St Just'. But there you have it Jake, the conflict between folklore and science. Fairies, ghosts, lights and enchantment, such themes passed down through the ages, suggest the only truth that generations of local people have seen unusual phenomena associated with stone circles and similar places."

I smiled at him and caught Aria's eye, "But you, Barnes, know differently. You're talking about a rational, scientific explanation. Is that it?"

"Of course, as to the lights, modern technology allows us to measure radiation, and the stones emit low levels. It can be detected by certain types of photographic emulsions, Geiger tubes and scintillation counters—and, Jake, living creatures can detect increased levels of radiation. On the whole, humans have lost the innate ability but some individuals...oh, but I could go on for hours, especially regarding the scientific side. Far better to get to the point..."

I nodded sympathetically. I could always research for more information.

"Please, go on."

He looked relieved that I appeared convinced. After what I'd witnessed on Bredon Hill, I was fascinated.

"I'll be as succinct as possible. I believe the megalith builders had a deep and intimate knowledge of their materials and environment and the relationship their minds and bodies had with them. Jake, the *physics of shamanism* belonging to thousands of years ago was more advanced than our twenty-first-century science from a physiological point of view. That's why I want *you* to be our modern shaman."

The bright enthusiasm in his eyes, enhanced by the angry black eye they'd inflicted on him, reminded me of the earlier fanatical light I'd noted in Aria. I'd almost forgotten his presence but now he spoke, and this time, his voice was passionate,

"Barnes is right, Jake, you working with us means we can revive the vital currents of the creative life force that lies behind our physical world."

I was conversing with two highly intelligent men but my uneasiness refused to go away.

"Always assuming I agree to throw in my lot with you. You'll need to be clear about my role, the dangers and who your leader is. Also, I should explain that I feel less than adequately prepared. I'll need some days of intensive reading. Do you have other books about the scientific discoveries, Barnes?"

He had. But he refused to return home to fetch them. Going over to the window, he pulled back the net curtain and peered through the chink.

"I'm being followed, so it's best if I bring them at night, say three o'clock in the morning."

"That might be dangerous, there'll be nobody about at that time," Aria said.

"Which is why you should collect them at the entrance to the Community Hospital. If they see me enter there at night, they'll only think it was their fault that I'm in pain. You park and leave one of your back windows wide open. As I pass, I'll sling a bag with the books in and nobody will be any the wiser. OK?"

"It's good, Aria conceded. Three o'clock then."

It all seemed very cloak and dagger to me, but Barnes's battered face should have alerted me to the extent of the danger we faced. At the time, in spite of my experience on Bredon Hill, my mind wouldn't accept the connection. How could ancient monuments possibly be a modern-day battleground? I was to find out, sooner rather than later.

EIGHT

TEWKESBURY, 2022 AD

The next morning, when Aria came into the lounge carrying a black canvas bag, I was poring disconsolately over the usual ordnance survey chart. The expression on my face alerted him,

"What's the matter, Jake? You look like you've lost a fortune at cards!"

I snorted and looked up,

"I don't like failing at anything I undertake." I pointed at the map, "Look here, I went straight past this when I was on the Mary trail. How's that possible?"

"Belas Knap? It's worth a visit."

"I'm not interested in a long barrow as such, Aria, don't you see, it must be on the Mary line and I missed it! There's Sudeley Castle too. I passed quite close. I suppose I was so concentrated on the flow that I detected that I didn't spot a deviation—as in the writhing of a serpent."

"Sudeley Castle? It's haunted, you know, by the ghost of the last wife of Henry VIII."

"Catherine Parr? That's interesting."

"Especially if the castle is on our ley line."

I'd already made the connection and was staring at the bag he'd put on the floor.

"I see Barnes made the drop off successfully."

"Yes, but I'm sure he was being followed. There was a grey car crawling along behind him but I don't think they saw him toss the books into my car. It was done so discreetly and they didn't check me out or follow me."

"Was the vehicle a Nissan?"

"Now you mention it, I believe it was."

"I thought so, it's probably the car that followed me from Castle Eaton."

"Luke Farthing?"

"And his sidekick."

"I must ring Barnes to see if he's all right."

I studied the map again, with the troubling thought that maybe I'd missed other *places of power* as I began to think of them. Nothing else leapt out at me, so I turned my attention to the serpent's head. I'd started from the tail. Where did the ley run from Pershore Abbey? There were interesting sites towards the west and my finger traced a line almost back down to Gloucester. I ended at a town called Berkeley, midway between Gloucester and Bristol. It lay close to the east bank of the River Severn and that made me think it would be an appropriate place for the serpent's head. The name rang a bell and I searched my memory. It came to me that the castle was where the imprisoned king, Edward II, was so atrociously murdered. I didn't know it then, but there were other more important facts I would learn about Berkeley.

It was decision time. Having settled for becoming involved in Aria and Barnes's hare-brained schemes—but were they madcap or was there a sinister truth underlying their mysterious behaviour? Had I thought the former, I'd already have left. I needed a plan for the immediate future and three things came to mind. First, I would study the material Barnes had given me; second, I would trace the Mary ley from Pershore to Berkeley; third, and the most important, I'd insist on a meeting with the *eminence grise*, the man pulling the strings of Aria and Barnes. I'd make him tell me who the real enemy was, Ishbel's boss or someone more powerful? I wanted to find out what they were planning. Of course, there was a fourth, even more, important thing—keep Jake Conley safe.

"Barnes got back unscathed. He told me he'd noticed the grey Nissan but after waiting outside his house an hour, he spied them driving away at half-past four in the morning. He sent a message, Jake, he says you should start your reading with *The Sun and the Serpent*, he says it's a classic and will clear up a few ideas for—"

"Talking about clearing up ideas…" I thought I'd wait for his reaction before exerting my mind-binding powers on him, "…I want you to set up a meeting with your boss. I mean, the man who's behind this business, the Aetherius Society fellow."

I watched his face closely and was prepared to bend him to my will when I saw his stricken expression, but then, the pleasant smile returned along with the intelligence in his green eyes.

"You're right of course, Jake, we've kept you hanging on long enough. I'm sure Lugus will be pleased to meet you as it was he who ordered us to involve you."

"Wait a minute! Lugus, you say, isn't that—?"

"Yes, the Celtic god of light. Incidentally, Julius Caesar identified him as equivalent to the Roman god Mercury or the Greek Hermes."

"Ah, the plot thickens! Hermes, you say, he of the wand?"

"Yes, but remember, Jake, Lugus is on our side. It's the Brotherhood who have misappropriated the wand."

"All right, but why does he hide behind an assumed name? I don't know anyone called Lugus!"

Aria laughed, "Not likely, is it? Well, I've never seen his face. He keeps his identity hidden from all the members. He always wears a mask. I doubt he'll let you see his features."

"I can cope with that, but if I'm to continue with this…whatever it is we must do…I insist on a meeting."

"Quite right, I'll see what I can do."

The next three days didn't fly by. I'm a great reader but Barnes had sent enough material to keep me reading for several months. I read the whole of the book he had suggested and found that essentially it dealt with the Michael ley running from near Land's End in Cornwall to Hopton on the coast of Norfolk. The authors had also discovered node points where the Mary current intersected the Michael trail and revealed these crossings to be ones of extraordinary power. Among the conclusions I'd highlighted, *Landscapes, where these nodes occurred close together, had been selected as centres of this ancient science of the dragon energies. At such places the serpentine currents changed their character, forsaking their usually gentle meanderings to assume coil-like contortions as if to contain the elements of the sacred landscape.*

I thought about this a great deal and began to put it together with other information I'd gleaned. I referred back to the eighteenth-century Lincolnshire doctor, William Stukeley, the remarkable amateur thanks to whose accurate drawings, we know the layout of the Avebury stones before many of them were lost to pillaging. The worthy doctor had a vision of the ancient landscape covered in a collection of Serpent Temples he called Dracontia, the greatest of which was Avebury. Believing stone circles marked important locations where the influence of the Earth Spirit could be concentrated, he identified a hidden network of 'veins and arteries' that channelled it into the countryside. My experience of tracing the Mary ley upheld this argument and, I reflected, it might explain why I'd missed some places of power, which could have been on branches, off the main line.

On the third day of my reading, Aria came to my room and said, "Lugus will meet you, Jake. It's arranged for tomorrow at three o'clock in the chancel of St Mary de Lode church in Gloucester."

"Really? Right, thank you, Aria. Excuse me, I want to press on with my research."

I waited until the door closed and then sorted among the many books stuffed into the canvas bag. The reason I'd given him was no lie because I wanted to check out the church. I'd passed it when I was in Gloucester but hadn't noted anything extraordinary. But I was wrong at the time as I now discovered.

The secretive Lugus had chosen it for a particular reason. Excavations had shown that it was constructed over two Roman buildings. The first, probably housing baths erected in the second century, was destroyed in the fifth century and replaced by a timber mausoleum containing three burials. This was destroyed by fire and followed by a sequence of buildings interpreted as churches, culminating in the medieval St Mary's. It is suggested that the original was a post-Roman British foundation before the Anglo-Saxons occupied this area.

In another book, I discovered that this church was the burial place of the legendary King Lucius, the first Christian monarch of Britain, and some believed, built on the site of a Roman temple. It also explained the strange name because Lode is from the old English word for a ferry and the Severn was very close by.

All this led me to believe that the choice of meeting place was far from casual and I wondered what this Lugus fellow was up to.

The following afternoon came, and I arrived ten minutes early, partly because I'm always punctual but also, I'd hoped to indulge my hobby of inspecting ancient churches and from my reading, I'd learnt that St Mary de Lode contained Anglo-Saxon features, not to mention that under the floor at the west end in front of the gallery is a trap door which when open reveals part of a Roman Mosaic pavement ten feet down and under-water.

My tourism would have to wait because Lugus was more punctual than I. The chancel was atmospheric with its lovely low Norman arch and white vaulted ceiling with stone ribbing. A solitary figure sat in the first row of wooden chairs placed before the altar. A lancet window with three lights of stained glass in the rear wall contributed only slightly to the dim light in the chancel. The gloom made the assignation more mysterious and along with the echo of my voice and the covered face of my contact, I felt as uneasy as he'd intended.

"Lugus?" I said and any nervousness in my voice was lost in the reverberation.

"Good day," and the head turned to me. It was too dark to make out the colour of the eyes behind the almond-shaped holes in the gilded metal face mask. The long straight nose and stylised eyebrows under the headband of intertwining scrolls represented the Celtic, Danu, earth mother. A highly symbolic choice as I was soon to find out. As for the rest of my interlocutor, all I can say is that his hair was brown, cut short and he was of medium build and wearing an expensive three-piece suit. A neatly knotted blue tie with thin white diagonal stripes completed his outfit.

"Mr Jake Conley, I presume. A pleasure to meet you, sir."

"Is the mask really necessary?"

"In my opinion, absolutely. I'm very careful to protect my anonymity and you may already have reason to understand that we're dealing with unscrupulous people who will stop at nothing."

Jake turned in his chair to glance towards the back of the church.

"It's all right," said the suave voice. "It's locked. For an adequate consideration, the custodian has obliged. Nobody can disturb us. Now, I should put you in the picture but first I must apologise, Mr Conley."

He proceeded to excuse himself for the subterfuge in luring Jake to Tewkesbury. Apologies accepted, he went on to explain the nature and aims of the Aetherius Society. Most of it made sense but at one point, he had to interrupt and express his astonishment.

"Let me get this right. You and your members believe the Earth is a living being? One of great wisdom and compassion—nothing less than a goddess?"

"Yes, and her name is Gaia, a breathing entity, extremely advanced and our ancestors realised this long ago. I can't explain the whole Aetherian programme here, in a few minutes, my friend, you must read about it yourself but with what knowledge you have of modern man—and I remember with indebtedness your successful battle against fracking—radiating love energy in gratitude to the Earth through prayer and other spiritual practices is the very least we should do in recognition for all that she has done—and continues to do—for us, unworthy though we most certainly are."

"Yes, I will read up on the Society. But tell me the reason you want me as part of your team."

I listened with unswerving attention for a full twenty minutes, interrupting very rarely for some clarification. When Lugus had finished, I said,

"I'll be honest with you, it's the first time I've heard of *devas* and never suspected their presence on earth. As for elves, don't be surprised, but I've had dealings with them and know the Queen of the Light Elves intimately. I've also come across the old gods, one of whom turned out to be an angel."

"My dear fellow, I think you're going to be of more use to us than I'd hoped in my wildest dreams. Now, it's time to answer your question about the Brotherhood of the Wand. Unfortunately, they are as knowledgeable as us about Gaia, but they are determined to debase and exploit the energies I have spoken of for their ignoble ends, which in general I can summarise in two words—greed and power. They know that if we can invoke sufficient spiritual energy, their despoliation will be over, their wealth diminished and their power reduced. The madness that is the inevitable outcome of unbridled lust leads them to espouse and promote war to further their aims. It is sadly, unlikely that they will allow a handful of men to survive having the audacity to oppose them when they don't blink at genocide. Let those words be a warning to you, Jake Conley. Now, you must go and I beg you not to linger to learn my identity—that would be a foolish move."

He signalled to the back of the church by clicking his fingers.

I stood and turned to go.

"Wait! Can we count on you, Mr Conley?"

I hadn't accepted his proposal formally but had no hesitation.

"You may do so, Lugus. It's a righteous cause. Goodbye."

"Goodbye, my friend. Your bravery will be well rewarded."

The custodian had opened the door and as I blinked in the outdoor light, I thought,

I'm not acting for personal gain. For once, Jake Conley, you are doing something you believe in, whatever the danger.

NINE

GLOUCESTER TO BERKELEY 2022 AD

On leaving St Mary de Lode, my forehead began to ache between my eyebrows, a sure sign of psychic awareness. But why? The answer was immediate as I detected the silver thread lowing away from the church. On my last visit to Gloucester, I hadn't picked up this particular course. Could it be the extension towards the serpent's head that I sought? I glanced at my watch, almost four o'clock, too late to set off on an expedition that would surely require considerable hiking. Thinking about that, my footwear was unsuitable for cross-country rambling. On the other hand, a return to Tewkesbury was reductive—a waste of time and a chance for the Brotherhood spies to follow me. I phoned Aria to say I'd be away a day or two and steered him away from questioning why. Then, I found a shoe shop and bought a pair of stout boots, suitable for my trek. Keeping them on, I strode through the city centre partly to break them in and also in search of a hotel or bed and breakfast. In Clarence Street, I located the Central Hotel and liking the look of the historic architecture, booked a room for the night.

Assured of a good breakfast, I retired to my room and dwelt upon everything Lugus had told me, running through it several times, straining to remember every detail. When I was sure that I'd forgotten nothing, I transferred from my armchair to the bed and lay thinking about him instead. The obvious and most striking element was his wearing of the Celtic mask. His choice, given what he'd told me, wasn't casual but that wasn't the point. Was his identity so important to go to those lengths to protect it? There could be only one explanation, Lugus, whoever he was, must be in close contact with the leaders of the Brotherhood and as such, they mustn't know of his involvement with the Aetherius Society or else—else, he would be in fatal danger. I'd not delude myself, that mortal risk was the mantle I'd assumed on agreeing to help Aetherius. Only that Lugus had no idea of the powers at my disposal, which included mind-binding, shape-shifting and, after what he had told me, knowledge of the elves. He had enlightened me about *devas* and their role in earth consciousness and in what Lugus called the *Great Law of Karma*.

I would need to invoke the presence of a deva and to that end, leapt off the bed, causing my head to spin by the sudden movement. This made me realise I needed to eat, perhaps my blood sugar levels were down. But so fascinated was I by the Devic Kingdom, I ignored my rumbling stomach and found the small paperback about earth power I'd brought with me. I'd been reading it earlier and remembered that south-west of Gloucester there was a standing stone where in times past, mothers would pass babies suffering from whooping cough or rickets through one of its larger holes.

I found the pages that interested me and read that in 1988, on a practical dowsing expedition, a certain Alan Lovejoy visited this Long Stone and used a Mersmann geomagnetometer on it. At the monument, the device registered a reading of seven on a scale of ten nearby and at the stone itself, the needle shot past the maximum in a band about one foot deep, some eighteen inches from the ground. Several dowsers laid their hands on it and the needle swung to level seven as the instrument rose up the stone. This suggested to those present that the water diviners had 'recharged' the rock, which indicated an interesting human-stone interaction. I thought I understood this better than them and noted the locality of the monolith, expressing the hope that my Mary current would take me there the next day—otherwise, I was prepared to make a detour. Now, setting aside these thoughts, I determined to go downstairs in search of food.

The next morning, I went to the nearby railway station and hired a locker to leave my shoes. They were an expensive hand-made pair of brogues that had cost several hundred pounds, so I was both reluctant to carry them around or to dispose of them. After this diversion, I returned to St Mary de Lode and picked up the Mary trail. It curved, as I'd hoped, south-westwards and I followed it out of Gloucester. My first stop was in the outskirts of the city in a village called Brockworth but before I arrived, I had noticed the disconcerting presence of another current, almost certainly the Michael flow. This was confirmed when the two currents began to run side by side and the masculine force became stronger until it reached the church, unsurprisingly dedicated to St George—the dragon-slaying saint. I couldn't resist the lure of my hobby and visited it to discover something of its history. The two forces blended exactly under the twelfth-century font. The building was erected in 1142 and two statues of Saint George stood either side of the altar with crocketed canopies to enhance them.

Outside the church, I had to choose which current to follow and since Mary wove on in my preferred direction, I followed her but after little more than an hour's walking, I was disappointed to revisit St Mary's at Painswick even if it gave me another opportunity to admire its yew trees. Here, Mary divided in two directions. I ignored the stronger line I had tracked previously and continued southwards.

A glance at my watch told me I had time to continue and the Mary flow wound round in the direction of Woodchester. I plodded on like a dogged bloodhound but the current by-passed St Mary's. This intrigued me but I couldn't resist a visit to the church, where a leaflet explained why the current hadn't passed there. It informed me that a Saxon edifice had been built in the northernmost edge of the parish over a pagan shrine, in 869 AD. Abandoning my inspection, I took up the trail and found strong evidence of the site when the Mary flow intensified and became strong and insistent at a certain location. I later learnt that archaeologists had found a Roman temple with a mosaic there. For the moment, I was thinking of food before pressing on.

After a pub lunch, the silver ribbon in my mind's eye writhed, to my surprise, eastwards and at the village of Amberley crossed again with the Michael current that, unsurprisingly, passed through the pretty St Michael's church. I didn't stay long because the Mary flow surged onwards to the east into open countryside and brought me to where I'd hoped, Hampton Fields, near Minchinhampton. I'd come about four miles from Woodchester and was feeling a little tired. The Long Stone was located on the Minchinhampton to Avening road about half a mile from Hollybush farm. It was set just off the lane with easy access. As I gazed towards it, I'm certain I saw a black dog standing near the monolith but, curiously, it vanished before my eyes. When I hurried over to the stone, there was no sign of the animal in any direction. A mystery. Putting this out of my mind, I inspected the rock. Some say it had been brought here from a prehistoric burial barrow. Whatever the case, the silver Mary current spiralled up around it decisively. I relaxed my concentration because I was weary and leant towards the stone, resting my palms on its rough surface. At once, a tingling sensation ran along my arms and pervaded my whole body. Like when a dog emerges from the waves and shakes the seawater from its fur, I shook off my fatigue. Feeling refreshed and intellectually perky, I had what turned out to be a splendid idea.

Deciding to concentrate again, but this time on the stone itself, I made a synergetic effort to interact with the megalith. The results by far outstripped any expectations. With hindsight, I'm sure the time of day helped me as there were no people around and no traffic. After a few moments of intense concentration, the air in immediate proximity to the rock shimmered as in a haze. Gradually, the vibrating cloudiness took an indistinct form. A column of light emanated from the stone and high above me was a radiant flickering countenance and two outstretched arms. I had no fear, rather a sense of calm transmitted to me by a being neither good nor evil. My feeling was that this presence was ancient, solid, permanent and infinitely wise.

The entity could read my tumultuous thoughts and spoke to me telepathically—something I had experienced with other beings in the past.

You are correct. I am a deva and you have summoned me from my kingdom. I have read all your thoughts and recommend that you fulfil your commitment to radiate spiritual energy for world peace and enlightenment. Never has the time been so urgent for an intense realisation by mankind that God is all and transcends this planet, His gift that unworthy men wantonly ravish.

"Can you help us?" Jake asked.

The Devic Kingdom responds to action with an equal reaction: to that which is transmitted by emotions. These, of late, have been violent expressions of hate, greed and other negative discolouration thrust upon the universal mind radiated through man. The diverse reactions, earthquakes, volcanos, tsunamis and the converse, natural harmonic peace are the result of the manipulation of primary energy by the devas.

"Is the Devic Kingdom in another dimension like Midgard?"

That is correct, my friend. Go seek the serpent's tail! You're in need of enlightenment.

The air around the monolith shimmered again and the towering figure faded to nothingness. My hands had remained firmly on the rock, but I felt a new sensation—as though I was channelling energy from some divine source through myself and directing it to bring about a predetermined end which was unselfish and wholly spiritual. That was my new mission. The quantity and quality of this energy—and also how well it is directed—would determine how effective my actions would be. As such, I believed this energy should be viewed as both natural and scientific—but a higher form of nature and science than contemporary orthodoxy was able to appreciate. All this in mind, I failed to take in that the deva had said serpent's *tail*. I stumbled on blindly seeking the head.

Fired by this conviction, I strode over to the wall, leant on it before taking the road and consulted the paperback about the Long Stone. Re-reading the entry, I was astonished to find a reference to a local superstition, which held that a supernatural black dog haunted the place. Not that it changed anything about my purpose but did rather confirm my psychic gifts for sightings. I concentrated and followed the Mary trail because I wanted to reach the serpent's *head*.

Refreshed in body, mind and spirit and, concentrating, I set off with the unfolding silver ribbon as a guide. I suppose I should not have been surprised when the Michael current began to interlace with the Mary because the serpent's head would be a significant node containing both elements, male and female. Therefore, it was no surprise when the two currents flowed parallel into a place called Cam, an outlying ward of Dursley. There, the church, erected in 1086, was dedicated to St George and to my delight, on the south wall of the tower was the carving of a very realistic dragon. The Michael flow surpassed the Mary in strength but the two crossed exactly where the font stood. But first, in the porch I admired St George slaying a dragon in the centre boss. Inside, the theme was repeated in a painting in the tower room and again in a tapestry of a St George and dragon banner in the corner of the north aisle. Was this church then the head of the serpent? No, it wasn't, because the two currents set off again out from the building, through the churchyard and away to the west.

I strode eagerly towards the River Severn. I had to take the Bristol Road and then cross Berkeley Heath. At this point, too concentrated to think of anything else, I noticed the widening of the currents and realised they were strengthening together as I approached the town of Berkeley. It had taken me an hour and a half of hard walking before I arrived. To my disappointment, the two currents flowed on uphill and I saw that they were making for Berkeley Castle and I was heading for dusk. There was no point in going up to the castle I realised because, anyway, it would soon be closing for the day. It was a fine sight with its formidable bastions and I noticed that there was a church tower standing alone just outside the walls. I hurried back into town, found a bookshop and bought guidebooks to Berkeley and the castle.

I needed another hotel and came across the central Malt House, which boasted a restaurant—just what I wanted. A quick shower and I was ready to begin my study of the guidebooks. For the moment, I ignored the splendid castle because I wished to know why Berkeley might be so important according to the deva. I put it down to my heightened spiritual state after absorbing energy from the Long Stone, but it leapt at me that Berkeley was the site of a power station, which had two Magnox nuclear reactors. This power station, the first commercial British reactor to enter operation, had since been decommissioned and all that remains are the two reactors encased in concrete. The administrative centre adjacent to the station was still active, however, the headquarters became Berkeley Nuclear Laboratories in the early 1960s and was one of the three principal research laboratories of the CEGB, the Central Electricity Generating Board. Surely, this had to be what the deva meant about man's mistreatment of the planet.

There was another unsettling detail—a local legend told that the town was once home to the Witch of Berkeley, who sold her soul to the Devil in exchange for wealth. It is said that, despite taking refuge in the church, the Devil carried her off on a black horse covered with spikes. I snorted at that, but the fact that a witch was associated with the place made me uneasy given what I was learning about the effects of earth forces.

My study of the castle was fascinating and threw up another ghost with reported sightings. No ordinary ghost this, but that of a king, for in this stronghold, Edward II was murdered atrociously in 1327. It was not so much this cruel episode that captured my attention, as I sat in an armchair after my appetising dinner, but the information that the castle contained the Chapel of St Mary on whose ceiling against Church regulations, the chaplain, a friend of the famous Wycliffe had written a passage from the Book of Revelations in the prohibited vernacular.

Even more importantly, outside the walls stood the tower of the former Abbey of St Mary on the site of an eighth-century Saxon foundation. I would explore this the next day.

As it turned out, the next day, it wasn't the church that mattered, but the uniting of enormous forces by the intertwining of the Michael and Mary currents into a great swirling node. I had found the serpent's head of Aria Gough's ley line. And I wondered whether this might be the site of a future catalytic event. This idea showed just how unprepared I was at that stage.

TEN

TEWKESBURY 2022 AD

THE EARLY MORNING SUN STREAMED THROUGH THE YELLOW curtains of the Gough's guest bedroom and filled it with aureate splendour. My body felt in tune with the glow and my mind incandescent after the encounter with the deva and the insight gained about earth forces. But how was I to implement this knowledge? There were too many gaps in my understanding and the books Barnes had provided made no mention of the surging currents I had discerned at Berkeley Castle.

Wondering how our forebears had invoked spiritual energy from such a site, I resolved to meet again with Barnes to exchange views and seek a way forward. For the second time, I contemplated the cramped space he called a lounge, cluttered with books and the bric-a-brac gathering dust. Someone once told me that the most ordered minds surrounded themselves with untidiness and vice versa. In that case, Barnes was a genius! He wandered back from the kitchen carrying two steaming mugs and looked in vain for a space to deposit mine.

"Thanks," I took it to prevent spillage and glanced around

unavailingly for a chair with a clear seat. Sighing, I took my tea standing.

"I came to see you to discuss progress. I've decided to embrace the principles of the Aetherius Society and wish to contribute." Outlining my perplexities, I explained, "I'm unsure of the ceremonial aspects and in any case, I fail to see how Berkeley Castle can be utilised for our objectives."

He sniggered in an irritating lofty way. I hadn't expected condescension from him. Somehow, his swollen lip exaggerated the sneer and made my hackles rise, but his words made sense.

"Berkeley? No, Jake, we must go to the heart of the earth forces. We're talking about Avebury! Prehistoric man was adept at reawakening the universal life-force and understood where and how to do it."

With a start, I realised that Avebury was William Stukeley's serpent's tail and I remembered the deva's words – I must seek the *tail*. So, Avebury had to be my destination.

"Okay, if I accept the where, the question is *how?*"

"That's precisely why we called you in, Jake. We thought you'd know."

I cast around seeking any notion that might provide me with a plan while my eyes roamed over the volumes strewn about the table, settled on an archaeology book and, with sudden inspiration, I said,

"That's what I need! an artefact from the Avebury area."

I told him about my retrocognitive experiences and revealed how I became transported back in time. After recounting some of my adventures—he showed particular interest in my Snape common escapade—then he began to rummage through drawers of rickety cabinets until with a shout of triumph, he brandished a stone artefact. I saw at once that it had a small oblong adhesive label on it covered in minuscule writing.

"Look here, Jake, this should do the trick! This came from a 1960s excavation at Windmill Hill in Wiltshire. You'll know that the heights overlook Avebury."

"What is it?"

"A stone axe...or rather an axe *head* because it would have been bound to a wooden haft."

"May I borrow it for a while, Barnes? If I can return to—" I hesitated, never having been farther back than the sixth century AD. He sensed my worry.

"If you're right about retrocognition, Jake, you'll be spanning over four thousand years."

"I know. It'll be the Bronze Age, won't it?"

"I wish I could come with you to 2000 BC."

"I've survived Saxon times but nothing prehistoric!"

He looked at me with undisguised admiration. Gone was the earlier patronising expression.

"I suppose you'll have to travel down to Wiltshire to make it happen but what a privilege to see what those people did at their ceremonies."

"Just as long as I don't become one of their human sacrifices!" He picked off the adhesive label, muttering "We don't want you going back to 1962, do we?" then handed it over.

"Thanks for this," I put the axe head into my pocket.

Next, like a wild boar grubbing in forest litter, he foraged among a pile of books in a dark corner of the room.

"Ha! Here it is, *The Neolithic World of Avebury Henge*," he read the title and flourished a battered paperback under my nose. "It's a bit worse for wear and I've scribbled some notes in it, but you might find it useful reading before you set off on your jaunt."

I slipped it into the back pocket of my jeans and took my leave.

I didn't get far because rounding the corner of his street, two ruffians blocked my path. Before I reacted, one of them grasped and pulled my arms behind my back. The other patted my jacket, checking what I had in my pockets. He fetched out the axe head but turned up his nose at it.

"Just a paperweight," he said, tossing it over a low wall into a garden.

I was too cunning to show dismay, "If you're after money, my wallet's in my inside pocket."

"Here, what do you take us for, common thieves?"

If I could distract them, I hoped they wouldn't notice the small Avebury paperback in my jeans.

"No mate," the scoundrel went on, "We've just come to show interest in your welfare."

"There's a surprise!"

"It would be better for your health if you steer clear of certain people."

"Ah, you mean Barnes Harper? It may astonish you, but that's my intention. He's an arrogant piece of work and I've just told him so to his face. I'd be happy never to see him again."

The two men exchanged glances. The one holding me released his grip.

"Just make sure you don't if you know what's good for you."

"Would you like to tell me what you've got against Mr Harper??"

"Not really. You'd do best to clear off from this town, Mr Conley."

No surprise that they knew my name.

"Well, my idea is to go home to my wife in Warwickshire - not that it's any concern of yours."

"You'd be surprised what our business is and be sure, we keep meddlers out of it."

I'd had enough of these reprobates and had succeeded in keeping my interest in Avebury a secret.

"I'll bid you good day then gentlemen since we have nothing to disagree about."

"C'mon, let's leave Mr Conley to get on with his life. That is, while he's still got one," he said.

The threat wasn't lost on me, but I wanted to retrieve the axe head. I thanked my good fortune that Barnes had removed the label from it. "I'll just recover my paperweight."

By the time I emerged from the garden with the stone safely in my pocket, there was no sign of either man. The only movement came in the bay window of the house whose property I'd invaded. To my relief, it was only a ginger cat on the ledge that was staring at me with shining amber eyes and no human knowledge of trespassing.

At Aria's empty house, I found Ishbel planting seedlings in their small greenhouse. I apologised for intruding but breathed in the heavy air laden with the scent of tomato leaves coming from the dozen vigorous stems, each a couple of feet high.

"What are you pricking out, Ishbel?"

I wasn't interested but wished to be sociable.

"Cucumber. I find it so refreshing on sandwiches in the summer and home-grown ones are tastier than those bought from the supermarket."

"Nature is so wonderful!" and I meant it more than ever after my recent discoveries. "Ishbel, I came to say goodbye and to thank you for all your hospitality. There's a little something for you on the kitchen table. I hope you like it. I looked for Aria but he isn't at home."

"You shouldn't have, Jake. You're the perfect guest. He said he was going to change the front tyres on the car, they're a bit threadbare."

"Will you give him my regards and tell him I'll be in touch."

I watched her closely for a reaction but ascertained none. Perhaps my imminent going away had quelled some of her anxieties.

I left a note for Aria thanking him and begging him to retrieve my shoes and placed the Gloucester station locker key next to it, also I'd added that I was taking Barnes's books with me on loan. I departed, carrying my backpack and two grips and walked the mile to Ashbury station. I knew I'd have to change trains. There were two transfers, one at Cheltenham Spa, the other at Birmingham Moor Street. Despite the changes, to my satisfaction, the journey was only a rapid forty-seven minutes. Feeling cheerful until I spotted a familiar-looking figure dart behind one of the broad metal poles farther down the platform when I looked his way. Unsure, still, I suspected it was one of the fellows that had accosted me near Barnes's home. I made no move as my train was arriving, but settled in my seat and through the window, as the locomotive juddered away, I recognised him staring from behind the pole, ensuring that I'd departed. This served to convince me more than ever that the time was right to leave Tewkesbury.

When I returned to Alice's loving embraces, she gave me time to settle before delivering her bombshell.

"Sir Clive rang. He wanted to speak with you but I told him I didn't have a contact number. I don't think he believed me, anyway, I thought you didn't want to speak with him. Did I do the right thing?"

"When Sir Clive Cochrane comes knocking it never brings anything positive. And yes, don't worry, I'll cover for you. It's probably the truth."

Both of us worked as secret agents and he was our direct superior, so I rang his Whitehall office at once.

"I believe you wished to speak with me, Sir Clive. I *do* apologise, I guess you must have rung when I was in the countryside in an area of no reception."

"So, you've been away? Alice said as much. And from what I gather, you've been upsetting some very influential people, dear boy."

"How is that possible? I've been pursuing my hobby of exploring remote country churches. I can't think of anything more innocuous than that, sir. May I ask who has complained and what they could object to?"

There was a long silence at the Whitehall end but at last, he said,

"Look here, dear boy, the person I'm talking about is one of the most influential people in the land and one I believe who would not appreciate his name being bandied about. As to what he's complaining about, I can only tell you that it involves energy. Does that mean anything to you?"

"Good Lord, I thought I'd put that old fracking story behind me."

The baronet's tone became abrasive,

"Don't play the fool with me. *You* know what this is about. I don't, to be precise. What I *do* know is that you'd better let sleeping dogs lie, old chap. This personage isn't to be trifled with and I wouldn't like to lose one of my most valuable agents. Do I have your word?"

I wasn't about to make promises I couldn't keep and my mind was racing to find a solution to this quandary. I decided on a reply worthy of Zhang Qian or, indeed, any ancient Chinese diplomat,

"I have no intention, sir, of rousing any recumbent canines."

I thought I heard the slightest snort on the line, but then his tone became jovial,

"I knew I could rely on you, old chap. Now, don't go wandering off out of telecommunications range, will you? There might be a job in the offing."

I groaned inwardly since his missions were invariably life endangering. I limited my response to "Right-ho, sir I won't," which was about as true as my earlier promise. I ended the call, smiling slyly, for I promised myself the next time I saw a stray fleabag dog lying soaking up the sun, I would not disturb it, but walk past sharpish—as usual.

I might have been flippant for a moment, but Alice's sombre face restored some reality.

"Sir Clive must be worried if he's taken the trouble to contact you, Jake. What exactly have you got yourself into this time?"

We sat and I explained everything that had happened since I decided to visit Aria Gough.

Alice's high spirits on welcoming me home were now replaced with a mirthless expression so out of keeping with her usual chirpiness that, against my better judgement, I agreed to let her accompany me to Wiltshire.

"At least I can cover your back, Jake. We'll act as if we're strangers, working strictly according to the manual. These people will expect you to be alone and if they try anything on, I'll be there to intervene."

Alice was a trained agent. I'd no idea of the degree of her

accomplishments, having fallen in love with a pretty receptionist at Whitehall. Since our wedding, I had come to appreciate her quick intelligence and judicious approach to problems. Alice would be an asset but I didn't want to expose my effervescent wife to danger. She mistook my reticence for my being self-contained and, absurdly, I found I had to explain my worries.

"You misunderstand, I feel like I'm putting you at risk and I'm afraid of coming over as patronising if I try to stop you. I know you are formidable, my love, but it's only natural I'm worried about you."

This speech made her feel better but did nothing for me but we'd decided and there was no turning back. I selected a map of Wiltshire —I had the complete set of 1:50000 scale Landranger Maps for the United Kingdom. I found ordnance survey charts essential for my hobby of exploring country churches, but, as now, they came in useful for an overview. I hadn't been to Salisbury Plain since my student field trips.

"Here's Avebury and a mile and a half away is Windmill Hill. I hope to be standing up there tomorrow. Look, the nearest village to them both is Beckhampton. Do you think you can find accommodation there?"

She worked on it with the Internet and made negative noises for a while before reaching for her mobile.

"How many nights?"

"Ask for three starting tomorrow."

Luckily, the only bed and breakfast establishment in the small village was happy to put us up.

"We'll go by car," I said, "It'll give us more freedom of movement and I'm sure public transport will be difficult in the area."

"I'll start to pack," Alice had rallied since deciding to come along.

The next day, on the drive down to Wiltshire, in a grave tone she said,

"I think I made a mistake yesterday."

"What's up?"

She scrambled for her handbag and pulled out the map, opening it across her knees. Sometimes, she has the irritating habit of not answering in words but actions. Out came her mobile,

"The Waggon and Horses? Yes. I wonder if you'd have a single room for three nights starting tonight? Yes, Conley. Alice. That's right. I expect to arrive around midday and perhaps you could reserve a table for two for one o'clock. Perfect, thank you. See you later."

"What was that about?" I had to ask even if it was obvious.

"I thought we'd avoid standing out as a couple if we had different accommodation. You can invent an excuse at the bed and breakfast for why you're alone."

"But if we're having lunch together—"

"We'll have just arrived unless..." she turned in her seat and studied the traffic behind us, "...you've noticed anyone tailing us."

"I *did* keep an eye open the first half hour and spotted nothing suspicious. So, we're all right for our meal. But I'm not sure I appreciate your staying in a historic pub whilst I'm in a guest house."

"I'm sure you can visit the Waggon and Horses in the evening but you'll have to keep yourself to yourself unless you find someone to chat up. It'll be interesting to see if you've lost your charm!"

She giggled but I found it about as amusing as the tearaway motorcyclist whose overtaking forced me to brake. After a string of foul language that especially my wife should not be subjected to, I needed to apologise.

"Sorry about that...but the young idiot could have killed himself, and us! Anyway, you're right. It's best to separate after lunch. We have no idea how efficient the Brotherhood's spies are and I'm a marked man."

The troubling thought also bothered me that my Porsche stood out as much as my public profile. I had become something of a celebrity after my bestseller and subsequent part in the archaeological find of the century. I'd already received some suggestions from film people about the latter. What chance was there my presence in Wiltshire would go unnoticed?

ELEVEN
AVEBURY, WILTSHIRE JULY 13, 2022 AD AND 2300 BC

On my third day in Wiltshire, I decided to make an evening trip to Windmill Hill. Taking the Porsche, I had to drive through Avebury, on to Bray Street, then make a right turn along a lane and find a suitable verge to park. This done at around seven o'clock, I looked around and, quite alone, climbed to the top of the hill. To reach the summit I passed through one of the ancient causeways over the deep depressions of the ditch. Once I had arrived, a magnificent view surrounded me, embracing prehistoric monuments—the imposing mound of Silbury Hill, still a mystery to archaeologists, the West Kennet long barrow on the skyline to the south and directly below, Avebury henge with its cluster of cottages in the centre. I spent some time absorbing the atmosphere and, for a moment, concentrated on the ley lines. I visualised two distinct silver ribbons in my mind running across the countryside, the Michael and the Mary, and as I stared down, the latter ran from the south past the hill and curved north to the church at Winterbourne Monkton before sweeping into Avebury. The Michael flow passed around the opposite side of the hill and took a more direct route to the entrance. As I gazed down, it was as if the two currents kissed near the stones in the southern circle of Avebury henge. Fascinated, I traced their separate routes out of Avebury, one of them, I wasn't sure which, veered through Silbury Hill, round to the Swallowhead Spring and on to the West Kennet long barrow, whereas the other took the West Kennet stone avenue from the henge and crossed with its partner again at The Sanctuary.

With my recently acquired insight into earth forces, I did not doubt that I was beholding the intersection of powerful energies at the holiest of sacred sites for prehistoric peoples. Soon, I would find out. I had come specially to admire the night sky from Windmill Hill but had not chosen the day for astrological purposes and it was only afterwards I realised that by sheer good fortune I had selected the night of the Buck Moon. The full July moon also goes by the name Hay or Wort Moon, but I prefer the reference to the emergence of antlers on the deer's forehead at this time of year. The disc rose in the east at 19.37 and what a mystical sight it was, catching the light of the dying sun, sinking in the west, it appeared blood-red over the horizon. How early man must have venerated her!

I didn't have long to wait to confirm this because my hand closed unwittingly over the smooth axe head in my pocket. My senses reeled and the air around me vibrated. When I regained consciousness, I was on my hands and knees registering the clamour of voices I could not understand. Retrocognition had struck again just as planned! The encampment was alive with hundreds of people and grunting pigs. Smoke prickled my nostrils from the many campfires dotted around the summit. I gazed down the hill where tough, lean, half-naked men were carrying pigs in litters. How strange to see swine treated like royalty not deigning to walk! Then a reason for this occurred to me. They had travelled many miles on foot to arrive here and they didn't drive their animals for fear of them becoming skinny and less succulent. I think it was the delicious smell of roasting pork that provided this revelation. Without doubt, I was witnessing a huge festive occasion. Spits were being turned not far from where I was standing and I heard the hiss of fat dripping into the flames.

One man nudged his companion and pointed down to the henge. With a start, I realised I was seeing the complete monument including the blue stones. My study of the building phases gave me an idea of the date, I was with Bronze Age tribesmen somewhere around 2500 to 2000 BC! Of course, at this time there were no buildings inside the perimeter but, similar to the top of this hill, three fires burned within the enclosure and several figures moved among the stones. I guessed from the gesticulating man nearby that they were the object of an animated discussion. I wondered if they were chieftains or shamans. The moon had risen in its entirety by now and was a delicate shade of pink. It seemed much closer to Earth here on Windmill Hill than I'd ever seen it.

Darkness soon depicted the sky in bewitching black, with the Milky Way draped like a necklace amid the various sparkling constellations. I turned to the south and there lay the long barrow, built, as I'd read, just below the rising point of the prominent giant star, the brilliant Alpha Centauri. The splendid heavens made me catch my breath. Little wonder that the primitive men around me studied the stars and probably knew more about their movements than I with my previously misplaced superciliousness.

The feasting continued in full swing as I sat and watched, unseen, and the moon rose majestic high in the sky, casting its wan light over the assembled tribes. I appreciated the amiable atmosphere; they had travelled far to be together to share the life force that pervaded all living beings, as well as, they believed, the rivers, stones and other places. But there must be more to their congregation here than simply eating and drinking and tale-telling, I felt. Soon, I was to know, as the moon reached its zenith, the massed folk knelt as one, staring at her creamy-silver face.

My attention was taken with the henge below, where the moon shadow struck the great stones of the Cove, and in the sudden awed silence of the hilltop, the rhythmic chanting of the men there made me shudder at its ritualistic lilting cadence that vibrated my eardrums like a pulse. I observed the horizontal axis of the moonlight aligning on the stones and then, to my amazement, beheld a vertical axis shimmer in the air above the henge. A collective moan came from the men and women on the hilltop, no longer staring at the moon, but all their eyes now fixed on the rent between worlds that I was witnessing and out of which stepped a larger-than-life female figure with flowing silver locks and dressed in a white robe. Before her, the men in the henge prostrated themselves and I knew I was privileged to see the Earth Mother in all her splendour, bestowing her blessing of harmony, fecundity and well-being on her devoted worshippers.

The White Goddess stepped back through the multi-layered axis and disappeared to awestruck sighs, everyone now hurried to make votive offerings. Whole joints of meat, beads, armlets and brooches were cast lovingly into the ditch surrounding the hilltop, undoubtedly to be found by archaeologists in the future—in my day, I thought. None of whom would believe, for a moment, encased in their scientific certainties, my account of the benign being I had worshipped along with these, our ancestors. Seeing the earth goddess had touched me to the depths of my soul and I enjoyed a spiritual and physical uplifting I'd not felt before, not even in the presence of the seraph I knew as Freya. This was why I had come and what I wanted to see.

Would Lugus and the Aetherians be able to reproduce the chant at full moon to invoke the earth goddess in the twenty-first century? I wanted to assist in their noble aim of harnessing spiritual energy to heal others in mind and body—and most importantly raise consciousness to help people to rise above the weaknesses of greed, materialism, violent emotion, hate, jealousy, and desire for vengeance. If this could be achieved, I looked around me, then my contemporaries would return to the state of harmonious coexistence I so admired here. Of course, I was not so foolish as to imagine that petty conflicts and outrages blighted some of their lives. They led a hard life, many died before the age of fifteen, but in their devotion and gratitude to Nature, they were, nonetheless, disposed to sacrifice and, in many cases, to undertake a journey of hundreds of miles on foot to propitiate the earth goddess. Instead, many of my generation, wounded and raped her without a second thought.

I bit my lip and thought with displeasure about the pollution and depredation of my century. As I did so, my head spun and the air around me distorted, returning me to an empty hilltop, ageless in its dignified silence under the stars. With anguish, I gazed down on the knot of Avebury cottages where the stones had stood and I remembered the tale of the itinerant barber, who had been one of a group whose fire and water had been applied to destroy the monoliths in the seventeenth century. Archaeologists had found his skeletal remains, together with the tools of his trade, crushed by the toppled stone he'd intended to smash. Had that been poetic justice or an act of revenge by the earth?

I didn't feel happy to be back in modern times as I considered how far we'd abandoned the values of our earliest ancestors. What I had seen this night would remain in my soul forever. I sighed as I contemplated the enormity of the task before me and set off down the hill towards my car, feeling guilty at the thought that it would emit exhaust fumes when I burnt the petroleum extracted from the depths of the earth. On the other hand, I accepted we all wanted convenience and an easy existence. We couldn't go back to a world without medicine and transport, I realised that but we could do away with the worst abuses and that would be my mission. There were people desperate to prevent me from succeeding to promote their odious ends. With that thought in mind, I slowed my pace when I saw a grey Nissan parked behind my Porsche—I'd been followed. What did they want? I hardly noticed a black Fiat 500, thirty yards farther back, practically hidden in the dark by its colour. As I approached, the driver's door of the Nissan opened and I recognised at once the man who had accosted me near Barnes Harper's house. He was pointing a gun at me.

"I warned you to keep your nose out of our business. But you chose to ignore our advice. How convenient you came here to the back of beyond where there are no witnesses to your demise, Mr Conley!"

My heart sank and I could think of no way of saving myself. Another voice, but female this time, broke the silence.

"Drop the gun or you're a dead man."

Alice! I'd know her voice anywhere. *What are you doing here? Thank God!*

The man spun around. He shouldn't have done that. The report of her gun and his scream both sounded deafening in the quiet at the foot of Windmill Hill.

I heard a groan, so she hadn't killed him. I leapt forward and snatched up his weapon before bending over to check the gravity of the situation.

"You'll survive! Good shot, Alice—straight from the training manual—*neutralise without killing*. But he'll need an ambulance and quickly."

"Help me put him in my hire car. I'll take him to Swindon Hospital to save valuable time. Marlborough's nearer but I don't think they have an Emergency unit. I can get there in twenty minutes."

"What about the police?"

"I'll ring Sir Clive. I'm sure he can deal with the local force."

"Except, Alice, he told me to drop this matter."

"I'll handle that too. Leave it to me!"

She roared off into the night and left me feeling extraordinarily blessed. The thug meant to kill me and now Alice was making sure he'd survive. I just hoped she was right about Sir Clive Cochrane. As I drove the short distance to my bed and breakfast accommodation, I wondered how the Brotherhood had known about my presence in Wiltshire? Or perhaps they didn't know. It seemed strange that they'd sent just one man to silence me. The usual method was to send a team. Was the wounded man a lone wolf, then? Had he followed me from Warwickshire? Surely, I'd have noticed him in my rear-view mirror. I'd been anxiously on the lookout for a grey Nissan on the way down. Now it stood by the wayside at the foot of Windmill Hill until its owner could fetch it. Another thought occurred to me: had Alice aimed as per the manual or had she shot to kill? Was she that accurate? I realised there was still a lot I didn't know about my wife, but how grateful I was to her! Then I thought again. A lone wolf wouldn't decide to eliminate someone. The Brotherhood of the Wand must have ordered my killing. If that was the case, I'd have to be much more careful in future. That organisation must be further advanced in their earth power schemes than I had imagined. Why else would they seek to prevent me from reawakening ancient cosmic forces?

TWELVE
PERSHORE ABBEY, 2022 AD

A mysterious phone call from Barnes Harrop sent me hurrying back to the Goughs where Aria explained the reason behind the urgent need for my presence.

"Lugus has been in touch with Barnes. You'd better sit down as this is complicated. It turns out that..." here he lowered his voice almost to a whisper—dramatic nonsense since we were alone, "...the Brotherhood meet at monthly intervals in the grounds of Pershore Abbey. They were there yesterday—"

"Mmm. The Buck Moon."

"Sorry?"

I smiled and looked apologetic, "Oh, nothing, it was a full moon yesterday. I was just making the point. The Abbey is on the Mary ley."

He looked anxious.

"Exactly! Lugus is worried and wants to know what they're up to at the Abbey. He says you, with your gifts, will be able to get to the bottom of it."

"The Brotherhood is dangerous. They tried to kill me yesterday."

"Good heavens! What happened?"

I told him about the grey Nissan and its gun-wielding occupant but didn't mention my retrocognition experiences. I thought it unnecessary at this stage.

When I finished my tale, he looked aghast, "Your wife must be a remarkable woman. Was she in the military?"

"In a manner of speaking, but forgive me, the less you know at the moment, Aria, the safer you and Ishbel will be. In fact, the sooner you tell me all the information passed on by Lugus the quicker I'll be on my way. I won't be able to do anything for thirty days, anyway."

"What do you mean?"

"The next full moon. The Barley Moon."

"Ah, of course."

He fussed about with glasses and a bottle of Lagavulin.

"Whisky?"

"It's a bit early, but why not?"

We settled in our chairs and sipped the excellent peaty single malt. I never tire of its pungent flavour and long finish.

"I must visit the distillery at Port Ellen, one day."

"It's on Islay, isn't it?"

"You should take Ishbel there on holiday. But tell me about Lugus's message."

"Barnes said to be sure to tell you that the Brotherhood doesn't meet *inside* the Abbey, but in the churchyard."

I frowned and must have looked surprised.

"That's odd. Surely, they risk being seen outdoors. Why would they do that?"

"I think I know, Jake. You'll be able to find out for sure, but I guess that the ley line doesn't run through the abbey." I was about to speak, but he hurried on, "There's a historical reason for that, in my opinion. You see, an Anglo-Saxon monastery was built in 681 AD on land gifted by King Aethelred of Mercia. It was dedicated to Saint Mary. The monastery soon became an abbey and it's had a chequered history. I'm sure you're interested but I'll limit myself to the essentials for our case. I have an excellent illustrated guide to the abbey you can read later." He paused and pursed his lips, "What was I saying? Oh yes, the Anglo-Saxons. Well, the abbey enjoyed great prosperity and the monks decided to build a stone building. They chose a site nearby so that they could continue monastic routine uninterrupted in their wooden construction. Sadly, Aelfhere grew jealous of their success in the tenth century and ejected them in 976. The abbey was restored by his grandson, Oddo, penitent for his forebear's misdeeds, in 983. He attempted to atone by gifting the bones of Saint Edburga to the establishment." He must have noticed my frustration, "Yes, yes, I'm getting to the point, we know that the relics were placed in a stone chapel in the church on site. Presumably, Jake, the wooden foundation had disappeared by then."

I nodded and remained silent for a moment. The conclusion seemed obvious: the seventh-century founders had erected their monastery on the Mary ley and the spot was outside the present-day abbey, where the Brotherhood of the Wand congregated at full moon. I wondered what nefarious business brought them to the modern churchyard. There was only one way to find out, but that would require me reconnoitring the graveyard. I needed to be based locally, but didn't want to put the Goughs at risk and since Pershore was a delightful market town, it would have ample accommodation. I took my leave and went off in search of lodgings.

Having found a suitable small hotel, I decided to revert to character and spend most of my time cooped up in the room. This served the double purpose of keeping me out of sight of the Brotherhood of the Wand and giving me time to study. I wanted to find out as much as possible about them, the Devic Kingdom, and the Aetherius Society. My disadvantage concerning both organisations was due to the vast gaps in my knowledge that did not affect their adherents.

My first discovery concerned magic on ley lines and I learnt to my horror that black magic today is not that different from the Middle Ages. Present-day symbolism is taken from such esteemed bodies as the Knights Templar, who to my surprise and consternation, still exist among us in a covert state. They also had a darker side unless their name had been deliberately blackened by the medieval Church, which I considered possible. I read with interest that the contemporary Church of Satan used the Sigil of Baphomet as their official insignia. The Templars were accused of worshipping this goat-headed demon as verified by the transcripts of the 1307 trial. I wondered whether the Templars were involved in the Brotherhood of the Wand, especially because, as my investigation revealed, the occult forces they strove to unleash and utilise were more easily invoked on a ley line.

After several days researching black magic, I felt as depressed as when combatting demons in the case of the Snape Ring. Since my salvation from the clutches of the Prince of Darkness, I had the deepest abhorrence and terror of the forces of evil. I had hoped never to have dealings with them again. It seemed, instead, that the Brotherhood of the Wand was forcing me to revisit my nightmares.

The date of the next full moon was marked in the diary of my smartphone and there was time to uplift my spirits by studying the literature of The Aetherius Society. How foolish of me to think it would cheer me! They believed the asteroid belt between Mars and Jupiter was composed of the fragments of what was once the fifth planet in our solar system. This came as a revelation and not a pleasant one because they argued that 60,000 years ago, there was a civilisation on this Phaeton, similar to ours, which self-destructed. And this happened even though the beings living on that planet were much more technologically advanced than we are now on Earth. The Aetherians feared that elements in our society, who sponsor war solely for profit, might not stop short of using nuclear weapons and causing devastation equally catastrophic to that which destroyed Phaeton.

I was very wary of pseudo-science and therefore reluctant to embrace the idea of this missing planet but when I looked into it deeply, I found that the ancient Sumerians knew of it and had named it after their goddess, Tiamat. Sumerian astrology has withstood the test of later centuries' accumulated knowledge. Why then would I doubt Phaeton's existence? Aetherian literature explained that the destruction of the planet killed its over 7 billion inhabitants. Phaeton was far bigger than the Earth and people living there were much more technologically and spiritually advanced than we are today. Despite that, it was destroyed. The Society went on to state: *we are all a part of God, but we also have free will and God respects our choices. So, it falls to us to choose to destroy ourselves or to develop into a higher spiritual community.* I couldn't help but agree with this sentiment and was grateful that a high-ranking official in the Secret Service, such as Lugus, held such views. I was still uncomfortable that I hadn't seen his face and that he continued to act through go-betweens. At least, now I believed that I knew what he and I were fighting for because, unless I was mistaken, a conflict was in the offing.

With two weeks to go to the full moon, I decided it was safe to pay a visit to the abbey graveyard. The day before my reconnaissance, I read Aria's guide to Pershore Abbey. Of course, I was more interested in the graveyard than the building itself for my purposes. I discovered that of the seventy-four graves, sixty-four were of airmen, among whom forty-one Canadians. One curiosity struck me as a very worthy sentiment: the town council had decided to name ten streets after ten fallen airmen. Originally, the plan had been to name the streets after varieties of plum, the fruit the town is known for. Much better to honour war heroes, I thought. Anyway, I doubted the Brotherhood of the Wand's interest in the graveyard was in any way connected to its occupants. Already, I was convinced they gathered there to exploit the earth force of the ley line.

The next day, I carried out my reconnaissance. As soon as I entered the churchyard, I concentrated on the Mary current and found it particularly powerful in a particular place among the graves. Looking around, I saw my ideal hiding place, from where I could keep an eye on that spot. The Brotherhood were sure to congregate where the ley flow was at its strongest. I was convinced that the original wooden Anglo-Saxon church had stood there. The place I'd chosen for concealment was behind an ancient gnarled tree with many low branches, where there was just space for me between it and a tall, square box tomb. At night, it would be impossible for any of the Brotherhood to spot me. I hoped there would be a clear night so that I could see *them* in the moonlight. My hope was for a cloudless sky on the night of 12th August.

My worry about the possibility of low light became an obsession. A few days before the appointed night, I came to a decision. Two years before, Freya had endowed me with extra powers. Among these, shape-shifting was the most exciting. At first, I'd transformed myself into a falcon and revelled in it by soaring as far as Ireland, but after the initial enthusiasm—I wasn't sure why—I'd grown reluctant to use this wonderful gift. I accept that I'm a complex character and subject to overthinking and this trait isn't always positive. Another person with the ability to transform would be doing so at the slightest opportunity but I had so many reservations that I hadn't sorted into a coherent argument against its use.

I confess that not only an obsession with light led, finally, to my decision to utilise the gift, but also fear. That's right. I was scared. The Brotherhood of the Wand wouldn't stop short of murder and, at the moment, I was enemy number one. The consequences of discovery whilst spying on their clandestine activity didn't bear thinking about. So, what creature might frequent a graveyard that if seen, would not arouse the slightest suspicion? One with superb eyesight and hearing?

I concentrated very hard on that animal and suddenly the hotel room was colourless. I could see only in black, white and grey. But how I could see! For the first time, I noticed the tiny, neat stitching around the rim of my bedside lampshade, whilst a hair on the carpet looked like a rope! It was enough to convince me, so I returned to my human form and as usual, pointlessly, went to check on my appearance in the mirror. Everything was fine—not a brown feather in sight!

Next, I checked out the creature on the Internet and discovered that in low light its eyesight was up to a hundred times more acute than a human's. That was the clincher, also because its natural habitat was deciduous woodland. I thought about the gnarled tree with its many branches, ideally located for perching. In addition, this bird had a three-hundred-and-sixty-degree vision without moving its talons.

On the evening of 12th August, at nine o'clock, I opened my hotel window wide enough for a tawny owl to fly through and shape-shifted. The owl isn't as acrobatic as a falcon but flies silently and effortlessly. I'd missed the liberating sensation of surging through the air and was disappointed when I reached the abbey grounds so soon. Resisting the temptation to prolong being airborne for pleasurable carousing, I swooped down to the tree and chose a branch that was neither too high nor too low: perfect for observation. The tawny owl is by nature patient and I found my usual restiveness quashed by my transformation.

Surprisingly, a tawny owl leads an interesting existence. It is aware of the slightest movement in the grass, which, to its acute hearing, makes a field mouse sound like a rhinoceros crashing across the savanna, so I had to restrain my instinct to swoop down and feed on the voles, shrews and mice I spotted. Towards midnight, footsteps thundered into the graveyard. As a human, my heart would have been pounding against my ribs but as an owl, I betrayed no such emotion.

The first two of the Brotherhood whispered to avoid making a noise but I could hear them as clearly as if they were shouting.

"We should put on our robes. The others will be here soon."

"What's this meeting about tonight?"

"The usual, I'd say...no, wait a minute! Didn't Zeena say the Magus would baptise a new initiate?"

I couldn't help myself, I exclaimed, "Kee-wick!"

"Shush! What's that?"

"It's only an owl or something!"

I removed all doubt, *"T-woo!"*

"Told you, it's in that tree somewhere."

He shrugged, bent down and pulled a black robe out of his bag. The other did likewise. When they had adjusted their garments, I recognised the white symbol on the right side of the chest. The Sigil of Baphomet—an inverted pentagram with a goat's head inside. Were they Templars or Satanists—or both?

Others arrived, each pulling a similar robe over his head. I noticed four women among the gathering of twenty. In the distance a church clock struck midnight. Luckily, that of the abbey did not, otherwise, I'd have been deafened; I'd read that its great chimes had been out of action for some years.

These thoughts had distracted me from the hush that had fallen over the black-garbed congregation. The reason was apparent because a high priest of sorts had arrived. This must be the one they'd named the Magus. His robe was covered in more symbols than he others, each with satanic significance, like the Leviathan crosses. It was easy to make out the stylised number 666 on one shoulder. It moved as he raised both arms in some sort of all-embracing gesture.

"Brethren," he spoke in a clear, well-educated voice, "we are united here tonight to participate in one of our most solemn ceremonies, a baptism. Step forward, Malcolm, and you, Zeena!"

I stared, unblinkingly, at the leader's face but in vain, because he'd covered it in white paint, which gave him a sinister gaunt appearance in the feeble moonlight.

I watched as he ordered, "Bare your arm, Zeena!"

She obeyed and he took out a small implement, which must have been a scalpel because the keen blade sliced her flesh so easily, leaving ribbons of blood in the form of an inverted cross. Witch blood for the initiation! The assembly began a low chanting as the Magus, with a skeletal grin, smeared the crimson drops, again in the same reversed shape, on Malcolm's forehead. The high priest intoned the ritual phrases, a perverted version of the Christian rite, eliciting the warped responses of the assembled cabal.

Without realising, my angry thoughts translated into hoots.

Cocking his head dramatically, the Magus raised a finger,

"Hark! How propitious! We have the bird of wisdom present at our ceremony. Malcolm you are indeed blessed."

The gathering broke into spontaneous applause, whereas I had to resist the temptation to fly into his smug face and tear at the white paint with my wicked talons. But what would that achieve?

I stayed still and ceased my hooting out of disrespect. A wise decision, indeed, because now I could listen to his uninterrupted speech.

Most of it was dull Satanic nonsense, but of course, my ears pricked when he talked about the winter solstice in Wiltshire,

"Brethren, we will come together with other believers at the serpent's tail during the solstice, reawaken Tiamat, the goddess of chaos, and distil the earth energy into potions. We can all profit from the Master's power. Allow me to demonstrate a small foretaste, tonight. I will summon my familiar. In this case, it was the most banal of familiars: a black cat. But there was nothing prosaic about it because around the animal's head shone a silvery aura. A similar emanation also appeared around that of the Magus. His followers did not seem surprised but when he cast a spell, his aura generated magical smut, which we all watched transfer in a scintillating arc to become absorbed by the cat's shimmering disc, darkening it. Gasps and murmurs accompanied this feat.

"There! It is done and will manifest soon in my increased health, power and wealth. I shall be ready for the great vocation! I'm not sure what'll happen to poor moggy!" He sneered.

His smugness was sickening and I needed all my self-restraint not to attack him.

"One last thing, Brethren, we have a dangerous enemy in our midst, whose whereabouts we must locate with urgency. I refer to the writer Jake Conley," I couldn't help but screech, "you see! Even our feathered friend, in its wisdom, is outraged at the mention of that name! Anyone providing me with news of the wretch's location will have *this* reward."

He held up a small bottle and a thrill ran through the assembly. What made the potion it contained so prized? I realised I would have to be on my guard and keep well clear of the Brotherhood of the Wand, of whom I was now a declared enemy.

THIRTEEN

TEWKESBURY 2022 AD

Call me old-fashioned, but I prefer my police inspectors not to have a bushy black beard, especially when they have a thin face, like DI Maddison.

He came back into the interrogation room looking for all the world as if he needed a good steak and chips, lowering his lean frame into the chair opposite and locking eyes.

"I must apologise for keeping you waiting, Mr Conley, but it's a devil of a job to get through to the people you need at MI5. Anyway, I spoke with Sir Clive and he corroborates your story."

"Story?"

"Oh dear, I'm putting my foot in it, again! Nerves, I suppose, it's not every day we work with a celebrity and a real-live agent. On a murder case too. Now, tell me again from the beginning..."

I sighed and fear I glared at the young detective. I reckon he was about my age, maybe a year or two younger, I'm thirty-eight. I watched him switch on a recorder and began.

"As I said earlier, I decided to go around to Barnes's – er – Mr Harper's house about ten o'clock this morning. I wanted to return a bag of books he kindly lent me and, frankly, I wanted some information about a certain individual. As you can imagine, when I arrived in his street, I saw a crowd of people, photographers and police and the yellow and black tape told me there had been a crime. With a sinking feeling, I hurried past an ambulance and asked one of your officers what was going on. He wasn't forthcoming, as you'd expect, and wanted to know why I was there. When I told him..." I paused for breath and considered how I would trim that bloody beard to make it more respectable.

"Go on, sir."

"Well, there's nothing more to tell. I mean, he radioed through to you, I presume and politely asked me to sit in his car, before he brought me here. You know the rest."

"I'd like to ask you some questions. What surprises me most is that Sir Clive knew nothing of your present whereabouts. Am I to assume that your current activities are unofficial, Mr Conley?"

"It's safe to assume that, Inspector. A curiosity on my part has become some kind of nightmare."

I could see his antennae prick up. He reminded me of a stick insect—do they have antennae?

"Please explain."

So, I did. Beginning with Aria Gough's letter until I ended with my graveyard visit last night.

He sat back with the look of a haunted man. He was justified, of course, this case would take him right out of his comfort zone and promised to involve high-ranking officials in GCHQ. With that beard, looking gaunt didn't suit him.

"Are you saying Mr Harper was murdered as a warning to you? By some kind of satanic cult?"

"Not simply as a threat, although I think there was an element of that, above all, to silence him. As I said before, he probably had the information I was desperate to learn. I'm convinced he knew or, at least, suspected, the identity of this Magus character, the leader of the satanic sect. I told you, he was very well-spoken—I'd say, public school, by his speech. Given that we're colleagues, in a sense, might I ask you to breach protocol?"

He looked thoroughly wretched.

"In what way?"

"Two things, reserved material. Was there any sign of this being a ritual killing?"

"Not at all. It was the rent collector who found him, by peering through his bay window. He saw Mr Harper sprawled across a pile of his belongings in a pool of blood and rang the emergency number. We rushed to his house and verified the murder scene."

"Untidy blighter, wasn't he? How was he killed?"

"I'm waiting for the pathologist's report but it looks like one of the three bullets severed an artery."

"Untidy? That's putting it mildly. But we believe he lived alone. Can you confirm that?"

"As far as I know, he did. So, no satanic symbols? Nothing?"

"No. You said you had a second question."

"I did. I wanted to know if you'd found a diary or anything that might lead us to those responsible for his death?"

"You'll understand that your evidence throws a whole new light on our investigations. I have men on the spot and I'll call them to do a complete search of the premises. If we find anything of the sort, I'd like you to inspect it."

I grinned at him. "I think you should know, Inspector, that the Brotherhood wants me dead."

I told him about my previous brushes with Luke Farthing and the unknown man in the grey Nissan. The policeman was less than impressed that I hadn't taken the registration of the vehicle but seized on my suggestion of checking Swindon Hospital for the identity, probably false, of the wounded man.

"We can lean on this Farthing character and may have to trouble your wife for a description of this would-be killer, sir."

"No problem. Here's her mobile number."

On the drive back to Pershore, I considered the errors I'd made.

Not taking the Nissan registration was bad but not following the Magus in my silent owl shape was unforgivable. I guess I must have been too shaken to think straight. I passed over a golden opportunity to discover his home and thence his identity. Would I be able to leave that discovery to the Tewkesbury police at the next full moon? Letting them earn their salaries and taking no risks appealed to me. With Barnes off the scene, my hope of recognition had taken a serious hit. Who was the secretive Lugus? How could I find out?

I turned the car around and drove back to Tewkesbury, where I found Ishbel in her greenhouse.

"Cucumber-ing?"

"Oh, hi Jake! You made me jump. Just watering them with a fine spray. Look, they're coming on nicely. See, the fruit's beginning to form," she pointed at a plant, "they're ninety per cent water, so I'll have to give them a lot to drink."

I couldn't care less but humoured her. Are you going to trellis them?" That was about the extent of my cucumber knowledge and even that I'd picked up from Alice.

She looked surprised, "Why, Jake, I hadn't put you down as a gardener. You're full of surprises!"

"My wife."

"Ah! I see. Anyway, yes, I haven't many plants, so I'll make a bamboo tee-pee and plant one at the base of each pole. Would you like a coffee? C'mon, let's go inside."

"Is Aria in?"

"Did you want to see him? I'm afraid he's gone into town for a flash drive or something."

That was a relief, "No, in fact, I wanted a word with *you*." Alone preferably, so they could talk freely.

Over coffee and a slice of her delicious pear and chocolate crumble, I asked her straight out,

"Aria doesn't know who this fellow who hides behind the mask of Lugus is, but I suspect you do, Ishbel."

She looked furtive and shook her head.

"I can't tell you! You'll have to ask Barnes."

Didn't she know?

"Barnes Harper died this morning. Someone shot him in his home."

She sat up straight-backed and darted a fearful glance at the window.

"Don't worry, nobody followed me here."

Her shoulders slumped and she clasped her hands in her lap, knuckles white. Eyes wet, she spoke with a tremulous voice, "I told Aria not to get involved. I suspected all along this ley line business would bring trouble. From what little I've heard, there are important interests at play. When it's a question of money—"

Voice faltering, she whipped out a tissue from her sleeve and dabbed her eyes before blowing her nose.

"You must tell me what you know. Ishbel. It's the safest course. The sooner we put a stop to these people, the more secure you'll both be. I'm in close contact with MI5. They won't let anything happen to you."

"T-thank God!" She sighed and added, "You're right that Aria and I don't know anything precise. It's just suspicions. Barnes knew, but h-he's *dead*."

She almost howled the word and wiped away a tear with the crumpled tissue. Luckily, she wore no mascara. Bravely, she continued, "Whenever they met, Aria kept me out of the room. He said that the less I knew, the better. So, I can't tell you much, Jake. But when I suggested Sir Francis Muir, our big boss was involved, I could tell at once by his expression that I'd hit on something—"

My instinct told me she had set me on the right track. Interrupting, I said,

"I'd like you to do something for me. Obtain a recording of your boss's voice. If I'm right I'll recognise Lugus."

She looked excited.

"I can do better than that! I made a video of his speech at Jason's retirement bash."

She hurried into the kitchen and came back with her mobile. She fumbled with the screen for a moment and thrust it into my hand. The wobbly image settled on a tall distinguished man with a thin face and lean build. The unmistakable voice...

"Ladies and gentlemen, it is my pleasure and privilege..."

I'd heard enough. I was listening to the cultured cadences of the Magus! The situation had worsened dramatically. I had expected to see and hear Lugus, this revelation meant that Aria and Ishbel were at serious risk by association with Barnes and, not least, me. They would need police protection.

"Would you forward me that video, please? Listen, warn your husband to be very careful in the presence of Sir Francis. He's the enemy. The same goes for you, my dear. You've been very helpful. I'll arrange extra security."

"Oh my God, Jake! Are we in danger?"

I gazed at her face, now drained of blood, her eyes wider and the neat teeth biting her lower lip. Her vulnerability made me wish to linger and comfort her, but I had to introduce some much-needed urgency.

"You'll be all right, Ishbel. I'll see to that."

The way I left the premises would not have reassured her as my eyes darted in every direction, seeking the most improbable hiding places. Confident that no spies were watching, without wasting time, I drove to the police headquarters. On the way, my mobile pinged. Ishbel had sent the video.

Seated across from him, I handed my smartphone to DI Maddison.

"This is the man who led the black mass, Inspector, and the person ultimately responsible for Barnes Harper's death. Mind you, it's my opinion and I have no proof. I'm also here to plead for protection for the Goughs. It's almost certain Muir will move against them if he took out Harper."

The police officer pulled at his shirt collar as if it were asphyxiating him. His anxiety was understandable. Depriving his overworked, understaffed department of two men delegated to protection was an unwanted strain on resources. Also, having to investigate, however delicately, the eminent personage of Sir Francis Muir was to threaten his career.

Fully understanding the situation, I suggested, "Consider passing the case upstairs, detective. I think it's a matter for the Chief Superintendent. If you like, I'll speak with him if you can fix it and maybe we can involve MI5. As you know, I work for them and if we can get Sir Clive Cochrane involved—"

For several days, I'd been considering phoning my boss. Aware now of the gravity of the situation, after Barnes's murder, I hesitated no longer. Right there, in front of the detective who was looking at me as if I were his winning lottery ticket, I tapped out the Whitehall office number.

"Cochrane, speaking."

In detail, but as concisely as possible, I told him where I was and what had happened since my arrival in Tewkesbury.

"Let me get this right, dear boy, you suspect something on a national security scale underlying this esoteric nonsense?"

"Whilst we're dealing with the occult and cabbalistic practices, sir, there's nothing fanciful about the earth powers I've discovered. That we're involved with people of Sir Francis Muir's stature is enough to raise our level of alert."

"By Jove, you're right! I know the bounder and for heaven's sake, he holds a key position in our hierarchy. We'll have no rotten apples if I have anything to do with it. I'll get onto the Chief Superintendent immediately, this case requires extreme caution, do you understand, Conley?"

"Indeed, I do sir, and thank you."

"Well done, old boy. Now, you sit tight for the time being. Nothing rash, d'you hear?"

"I do, sir."

The call ended and I gazed at Maddison.

"I can't tell you how relieved I am," he said. "All I have to do is wait for instructions from the Super."

"Come on!" I screamed in his face, "You send some of your chaps round to the Goughs this minute!"

Anguished, he looked sheepish too, "You're right of course, his Lordship can hardly reprimand me for taking precautions. I'll see to it at once."

Driving back to Pershore, I realised that my Porsche was far too recognisable, so I found a bay and paid monthly, in a carpark in the aptly named The Parks for £75 a month. If I needed a vehicle, I'd hire one, but for the foreseeable future, I meant to obey orders, lie low and wait or the harvest moon in September.

FOURTEEN

WHITEHALL, LONDON 2022 AD

"Would you say a man is better off knowing his enemy than not knowing his friend, sir?"

I studied the well-manicured hands that momentarily stopped twirling and clicking a retractable ballpoint pen. Sir Clive Cochrane for once, was caught off-balance. Whenever, rarely, that happened, as on this occasion, he answered with a question to gain time.

"Is that why you've come down to London, with that query, old chap?"

I knew the ploy and he was off again, twirl-click-twirl.

"It is, sir. You see, my life is in danger and although I know who my potential killer is, I have no idea of my possible saviour. It's not the most relaxing of situations as I'm sure you'll appreciate. That is why I thought it best to involve the Department and, in particular, yourself."

"Me, dear boy? Well, that would suggest you consider this chappie, whoever he is, to be a threat to national security."

"I believe he is and maybe one whose tentacles stretch beyond our shores."

"By Jove! You'll be telling me you want MI6 on this too."

The clicking had even surpassed the twirling in velocity—but there was nothing rapid about his speech or his unwavering gaze. Those steely eyes had probably unmanned sterner interviewees than poor pusillanimous Jake Conley.

"I think you'd better put me in the picture; if I know anything at all about you, my lad, it is that you are not prone to exaggeration. And how is the delightful Mrs Conley?"

He fired off the occasional unconnected question to catch a fellow off guard and to attempt a passable semblance at humanity, however weak.

"Thank you for asking, but I've been away for several weeks and when we last spoke, she seemed well enough, enthralled as usual in her manuscript analyses."

"Hmm, yes, she's making quite a name for herself in that field—I keep informed, you know. A bright gal," he pronounces it 'gell', "but of course, we always knew that. Now, as for your little matter…"

He raised a languorous eyebrow, steepled his hands, leant back and rested his head, eyes half-closed, on his high-backed leather chair. I knew his sharp brain was taking everything in about the Magus, even if he looked comatose. When I'd finished my account with, "… it's just that I don't understand to what purpose—" he snapped into steely-eyed mode again and said,

"Mmm, Sir Francis Muir. I told you I knew the blighter—*you called him bounder before and a rotten apple*—and, naturally, as he's one of ours. There's an extensive dossier on him. Now, I'm about to adopt your opening gambit, dear boy, would you say a man is better off knowing things that might endanger him or being kept in the dark for his safety?"

"A man cannot have more than his life to lose, sir, so I'd opt for the former, however unwisely."

"In that case, whilst I decide, why don't you tell me what little you know about your so-called friend in this affair?"

I explained about the strange masked encounter in the chancel of St Mary de Lode church in Gloucester, throwing in my suspicion that Lugus was a high-ranking official in GCHQ. My additional opinion that his aims as expounded to me appeared, at face value, to be noble, caused the slightest raising of an eyebrow. I rambled somewhat about The Aetherius Society, none of which seemed to interest my employer until, by connection, I described my experience at the Long Stone. My word, how he sat up then! The ballpoint went into action for its true purpose as he scribbled notes into his familiar black notebook.

"And you say the monolith *exerted* a force that threw the villain right off his feet?"

"I can assure you, that is what happened."

"Well, I never! Do you know," again the disconcerting change of tack, "I think I have no choice but to dispense with protocol, Jake. You are far too great an asset to keep ill-informed. What I am about to tell you will put you at great risk and, it goes without saying, is of the most sensitive nature. Not even your lady wife may be apprised of it." The implacable gaze bored remorselessly into mine until quite satisfied that he observed unswerving obedience.

"Sir Francis Muir serves the Crown, Jake. But not the crown as you understand it—not the British Monarchy. The cad is as near to a traitor as you can get whilst not overstepping the line, together with his oligarchic cronies. The man is a Freemason and Knight Templar. Ah, I see you're surprised, my friend, but the Templars are among us, as hale and hearty as ever! The Crown, as I mean it, is the Inner City of London, which is an independent State in London belonging to the Vatican system. It is a banking cartel which has ramifications around and beneath that hide its true power. The City is the Knights Templar Church, also known as the Crown Temple or Crown Templar, and is located between Fleet Street and Victoria Embankment. The Temple grounds, as you may know, are home to the Crown Offices at Crown Office Row."

I sensed that my mouth had dropped open and made an effort not to gawp, like an idiot. Even for one as acute as myself, it was a hell of a lot of Crowns to take in! With astonishing equanimity, he continued to deliver his devastating exposé.

"The Crown Temple controls the Global legal system, Jake, including those in the United States, Canada, Australia, and much more; this is because all Bar Associations are franchises of the International Bar Association at the Inns of Court at Crown Temple based at Chancery Lane in London." He began twirling and clicking the pen again. I think he needed to soothe his nerves at imparting shattering news. "All Bar Associations are franchises of the Crown and all bar attorneys or barristers throughout the world pledge a solemn oath to the Temple. I wonder how many are aware that this is what they are doing. Bar Association 'licensed' solicitors and barristers must keep to their oath, pledge and terms of allegiance to the Crown Temple if they are to be *called to the Bar* and work in the legal profession. Would you believe, dear boy, that the ruling Monarch is also subordinate to the Crown Temple? This has been so since the reign of King John, in the thirteenth century when royal sovereignty was transferred to the Crown Temple and, through this, to the Roman Church."

"B-but...what you're saying is that there's an independent state in our land. Surely, that's impossible!"

Also, it seemed inconceivable that his eyes had become harder? But they had.

"Have you listened to a word I've said, Conley? Not only is it possible, but it's also a frightening deception we're forced to tolerate daily. You must have noticed that the symbol of the Inner Court is a white Pegasus on a starburst background? If you do your homework, you'll discover that it is the symbol of the Jesuit Order, not to mention of the Order of the Garter, the Crown Corporation and the American Council on Foreign Relations. I think you will need to study your enemy in considerable depth."

"I know quite a lot about the Templars, sir, but I had no knowledge of this oligarchy. What are its aims?"

"Nothing less than a single-state world government! They have been laying the foundations for many years. I won't put your life at infinitely greater risk by revealing the identity of the eminent man who declared that for this to happen eighty per cent of the world's inhabitants would need to be sacrificed—eliminated within two generations. They aim to move us into a post-industrial world where nation-states are eroded to favour a *one-world electronic feudalism.* Only an elite, what he calls the 'Brain Lords', will prosper and enjoy the fruits of technology. The rest of the survivors will be doomed to a life of misery."

"But people won't accept that! It's a nightmare you depict!"

"My dear fellow, it's well underway, the British financier oligarchy has gone to considerable pains to foster a sex, drugs, rock and roll counterculture. Thanks to that great writer, Aldous Huxley, we even have a term for it—*the concentration camp of the mind.*"

I was stunned by this outpouring and numbed by the irrefutable logic. I could see it in the manipulation of the media, in the trash put out for mass consumption and the exploitation of fake news. I felt decidedly ill.

He must have recognised the effect of his words on me because he reached for two glasses in a cabinet near his desk and poured two generous single malts.

"Lagavulin, your favourite, I believe."

If ever I needed one! My torrent of questions could wait as I savoured the fiery liquid on my palate.

The desired effect achieved, I sat back fortified and resolute—ah, the power of Dutch courage! I blurted the burning question,

"If Sir Francis Muir is so well-installed in this organisation, what on earth is he doing in a graveyard, conducting a black mass?"

"You see, dear boy, how necessary it is to know your enemy! A little history won't go amiss here. The Templars to give them their misnomer: the poor fellow-soldiers of Christ and the Temple of

Solomon. *Poor?* Ha! The Templars accrued immense wealth and power and in the Middle Ages owned over nine thousand manors across Europe as well as the majority of mills and markets. They issued the first paper money and became the first European bankers. When they were accused of devil worship and persecuted, they allied with the Freemasons, who gave them refuge. Their satanic practices are well-documented and, whilst much Church-State propaganda must be ignored, there's never smoke without fire, dear boy. I strongly recommend you read the 1307 trial transcripts so that Sir Francis Muir's activities become clearer."

"Satan worship for power and wealth," I mused, "but there's more to this and it involves earth forces."

"Ah, that's where you come in, old chap. I can't help you there. Find out what the devil—ha-ha, literally! — he's up to. That's an order."

"Yes, sir, but I'm going to need assistance. What about this Lugus fellow?"

As an employer, Sir Clive, so cultured and sharp, had two personae: the cold, intimidating master of all he surveyed and, alternatively, the warm, effusive complicit friend of his agent. The former mode kept his subordinates on the straight and narrow, whereas the latter, gained him unwavering devotion, but he was wise enough to use it sparingly and held it back for when, as now, it became necessary. His tone grew gentle and persuasive,

"What did you glean of the person behind that mask? Sex? Age? Accent?"

"Male, mature, middle-aged, sophisticated, and he spoke in received English."

"Are you sure he's in GCHQ?"

"The Goughs and poor Barnes Harper led me to believe so."

He sat back and slid pen and notebook away from where he placed one hand over the other. Looking over his lightweight spectacles, he said,

"I know who Lugus is. You'll need his help but can't blow his cover by walking into his office. Leave this to me, dear boy. He's an old friend and I'd trust him with my life."

I don't believe you'd trust anyone, you old fox!

This is a terrible habit of mine. I go off into a world of thoughts of my creation and become distracted.

My boss saw that, frowned and said cuttingly,

"Presumably a penny is far too small an amount for such profound reflections?"

I smiled but the moment was critical, I needed all the help available.

"Sorry, sir. I was just thinking that someone you trust implicitly would be exactly what I desperately need."

"Ah, yes, indeed! There's no harm in telling you his identity except it must not be divulged, as you'll appreciate and you'll wait for *him* to contact you. He is Sir Samuel Blackwell and practically commands the whole of GCHQ. He's Muir's overlord and will be less than impressed with his underling's despicable activities. Sir Samuel is a patriot and as you have established, a man of extremely high principles. I had no idea he had contacted you, dear boy, else I'd have been involved earlier. It seems you came to his attention based on your extraordinary gifts, which make you an indispensable member of MI5."

"Thank you, sir. I imagine he has eyes and ears everywhere and will have found me through the Goughs and their late friend."

"That's very likely. I'll get in touch with him right away. Meanwhile, sit tight, keep a low profile. Oh, and mug up on the Templars, dear boy! That'll be all for now. My best regards to your lady wife."

Heaving open his padded door, always a test of my arm strength, I exited deep in thought. Every encounter with Sir Clive Cochrane left me feeling like a condemned man in the dock. All my boss lacked was a powdered wig and a black cap. Never more than on this occasion had I felt like a doomed man walking through that door. How could an insignificant would-be novelist turned psychic investigator combat the clandestine activities of a ruthless sect of money men? With every leaden step out of the Ministry building, I knew the impossible had to be achieved, not just for the sake of my country, or of the world, but also those worlds hidden to our eyes behind a veil.

FIFTEEN
COOMBE HILL, GLOUCESTERSHIRE, 2022 AD

The choice of *The Swan* in Coombe Hill reflected a fair-mindedness on the part of Sir Samuel Blackwell that I was later to appreciate to the full. This roadside inn, under the painted sign of a white swan with outspread wings, located four miles equidistant between Tewkesbury and Cheltenham, was within easy reach for us both.

Sir Clive had relayed me the time and venue and so began his role of intermediary. To arrive at the Swan, for purposes of anonymity, I opted for a nondescript hire car. My boss, knowing my preferences also added, "It's a CAMRA place, you know, and they voted it Pub of the Season last year. Just your cup of tea, dear boy, or should I say..." I'll leave his quip unfinished, just as it deserves! But the ale was worthy of its awards and Sir Samuel had chosen time and place well because the only other occupants of the elegant lounge, over in the opposite corner, were far too lovestruck to spare a thought for two unexceptional men—I refer, of course, only to superficial external appearance. I believe Sir Charles must have raided a theatrical props box to find such an unengaging well-worn beige raincoat. I could tell after a few words that this shabby façade was a sham; Sir Samuel, I was soon to realise, possessed one of the most acute and implacable brains it has ever been my privilege to meet.

He wasted no time getting to the point,

"You will understand that the Brotherhood of the Wand must believe and suspect nothing other than that I am one of their most important and loyal members."

I'm afraid I couldn't restrain a gasp.

"I see you have a sharp mind, Mr Conley. You caught on at once to the precarious nature of my position. Well, drastic times call for extreme solutions. That's why nobody except Clive Cochrane and the two of us must know."

I didn't fail to register the omission of the honorific title—*these are old buddies. They probably went to the same school.*

Almost as if those sharp grey eyes could read my brain, he said, "Clive and I go back a long way, so, as long as you are careful, Mr Conley, my role as a double agent is safe."

"You have my word, Sir Samuel."

The thin lips curled into a pleasant smile,

"I've done my homework, Jake. I'm going to use your given name. I presume you don't object?"

"Not at all, Sir Samuel." I was beginning to like this man who appreciated good ale.

"You'll want to know precisely what's going on. It may be worse than you already know, I'm afraid. The Brotherhood of the Wand?"

He said that as if I'd asked a question, which I hadn't, I'd simply loaded a machine-gun clip full of them and was holding my fire. But he was so concise and lucid that I would not need most of them.

"Their idea, Jake, is to summon the sleeping forces of Nature and use them to bring about another Ice Age, which they will cause to prevail for five years, long enough to eliminate eighty per cent of the world's population. They have inbuilt into their masterplan their means of resisting the severe climate so that in one fell swoop, they have solved the problem of global warming and overpopulation."

"I don't see how they can bring about this Ice Age."

"Do you not? Well, consider that your so-called *primitive man* worshipped the earth goddess and begged her to overcome the serpent—the dragon—whatever you wish to call it. In so doing, she ensured a natural balance that humanity has enjoyed for centuries…" The steely eyes bored into mine to see if I was following and convinced, which I was. "…The Brotherhood seeks to reawaken the dragon and in invoking it at the winter solstice, will unite to it diabolical forces to subdue the goddess into a submission such that darkness will reign and the onset of perma-winter will come about. In this way, they will not need to employ nuclear weapons and the devastation and radiation it would inevitably entail. They will quell the dragon after five years and rely on the earth to regenerate."

"What kind of world do these *Brain Lords* wish to reign over?"

"Why, my dear fellow, a subservient dystopian one: one where people are begotten solely with a single purpose and, that is, to make their rulers richer, happier, more comfortable and uniquely privileged to enjoy the bounty of a resurgent Nature."

"They're crazy! People will rebel. They won't permit this insanity."

Sir Samuel looked at him pityingly,

"Sadly, you are quite wrong, Jake. They are not mad but coldly sane and calculating. You speak of people and rebels in those terms because you are measuring by your yardstick, not theirs. They have foreseen *everything*. They plan to create *The Mall*—an artificial environment which none will ever leave, nor wish to do so. It will be populated by laboratory babies from sperm and egg banks: genetic material collected from the Brain Lords themselves. The offspring will be reared with no knowledge of the outside world, no history or geography, no culture of any kind will penetrate their consciousness. Their brains will be filled with scientific learning and their task will be to improve the technology considered of service to the Brain Lords. There will be no language except English and that will be restricted to technical vocabulary. Jake, they will know nothing of sexual attraction and will not reproduce."

"This is diabolical! So, mankind is destined to extinction."

"Of course not, the overlords have factored that in too. Among the scheduled survivors of the Ice Age will be young healthy women selected for their beauty and intelligence. Their personal data has been collected across five continents. The Brain Lords will move with speed and precision in January and unless we can stop them, Jake, the world as we know it is doomed."

"How sure are you, Sir Samuel, that the Brotherhood can reawaken the dragon?"

"How convinced are you of the strength of the earth forces you have discovered?"

"My findings are limited. I have experienced the energy at the Long Stone in Gloucestershire and was impressed."

Sir Samuel made a moue,

"Peanuts! Multiply that a thousandfold! Avebury is on the Michael line that extends across the North Sea into Europe—need I say more?"

My forehead ached intolerably and I put both hands to my head.

"I say! Are you all right, dear chap? You look frightfully pale!"

"I think my head is going to explode with what you've told me, Sir Samuel. These fiends have to be stopped. But how?"

"That is where you come in. You possess extraordinary psychic powers or so Clive Cochrane tells me."

"Me? Against all the might of the City, its Templars, Satanists and fanatics? How can I hope to succeed?"

"You are not alone. We'll devise a plan, but to do that, you'll need to infiltrate them thoroughly."

"That should be the easy part, Sir Samuel. I can go wherever I want, quite unseen."

The mandarin looked sceptical for less than two seconds,

"You know, I believe you *can*. In that case, I think it's safe to say that if we can maintain secrecy, you'll be able to call on the might of the British armed forces at the right moment, of course. The logistics of that, you'll leave to me. Not a word to anyone, old chap. Only

Clive may know of our plans and about whose side I'm on. If you need me, contact him."

I remained seated and deep in thought in the lounge bar after Sir Samuel Blackwell had left. The young couple in the opposite corner barely glanced at me, absorbed as they were in each other. I rose unsteadily, not due to the two beers I'd enjoyed, but more to shock. I needed something stronger and although the woman behind the counter couldn't provide me with Lagavulin, she had an unopened bottle of Royal Lochnagar.

I'd not had the pleasure of tasting it before, so ordered a double—something I didn't regret from the first sip. When a man is shocked, dismayed, anxious and distraught, a warm spicy aroma and a taste to savour, can go a long way to remediating the situation. Not a connoisseur, I rolled the liquid around my palate and tried to interpret what my senses were telling me. Was that a hint of fruit and malt? Maybe vanilla and oak? Yes, I was sure and enjoyed the sweet long-lasting finish as I contemplated the name, Royal Lochnagar. *I'll bet it has something to do with Balmoral.* This was only conjecture, but when I decided to check with the Internet, I discovered that the distillery was close to Balmoral and that the founder, John Begg, had dared to invite the family of Queen Victoria and the sovereign to sample a 'wee dram' of his new brew in 1848. The impressed monarch granted the privilege of calling the whisky, *Royal*.

And am I going to permit the Brotherhood to gain exclusive rights to the best things in life? I am not! I'd rather die than let them achieve their evil goals.

Just how I was going to stop them, I didn't yet know. The one certainty was that very soon I'd have to become a tawny owl again.

SIXTEEN

PERSHORE ABBEY, SEPTEMBER 2022 AD

Some people call the tawny, the *screech* owl, and if ever I felt like screeching it was this September full moon under the scudding clouds as I perched in the same tree as on my previous visit to the Pershore Abbey graveyard. The intermittent wan moonlight filtered through its branches to chequer the cheerless graves. At moments I half-expected a ghastly apparition to emerge from the dumb turf because my brain was reeling with thoughts of skulls, coffins, epitaphs and worms. Were the venerable dead, in the gloomy horror of the grave, whose youthful blood, spilt to defend freedom, somehow looking down on my efforts to emulate them? Never had I felt as vulnerable as in that churchyard, where silence reigned until rent by the caw of a raven high on the abbey tower—the call of the bird of death.

Unlike the last enemy to threaten our way of life, the Brotherhood of the Wand operated from within, but they shared the same ideal of seizing total power. They both vaunted an insignia: the former wore the swastika, the latter, the Sigil of Baphomet. My large amber eyes stared unblinking at the emblem recurring on the black robes congregated beneath my tree. To deferential silence, the Magus arrived—Sir Francis Muir to my knowledge—but incognito to those gathered below me. His thin face painted as before, sallow as a church candle, might well have emerged from a melancholy vault. Never having had the misfortune to meet him, I supposed his disguise to be effective.

One should not pretend respect from a person such as the Magus, so it didn't surprise me when he clambered to stand on a box tomb, creating a commanding position over the assembly. The stone chest happened to be where the earth forces were at their strongest. Amid reverential quiet, he addressed his attention to the expectant upturned faces of the black-robed gathering, raising his arms and beginning,

"Brethren, three months separate us from our place in history. I have an announcement this evening that will rank among the most stirring call to arms uttered in this land over the centuries. We need to prepare no weapons nor risk our lives, my friends. As your initiation requires, the service of mental energy will suffice. It is my privilege and honour to advise and organise you for the moment we have waited a lifetime to arrive."

These words were met by gasps, whispers, nudges, nods and grim smiles all in total harmony with the overriding cheerless hush enveloping the moot.

"You will travel independently to Avebury, near Stonehenge in Wiltshire, one day before the winter solstice. We shall gather within the henge on the evening of 21 December, where we will be joined by fellow brethren from other chapters of our noble Brotherhood. Together, using the powerful earth forces that run through the site and chanting our invocations, we shall reawaken the serpent and bring her forth after millennia of slumber. With the help of our Master, she will devour the earth goddess. It may shock you to know that we will have chosen to go against Nature, causing sickness across the planet," his voice rose in exaltation, "life will become drab and colourless, but do not fear the oncoming dark age because you, the elect, will enjoy the beginning of the Great Return—what will be a Golden Dawn shared only by the few."

Complete and total fanatical madness! I couldn't refrain and hooted as much. The Magus spun and pointed to my tree.

"The bird of wisdom once again blesses our encounter! The ancients had their omens, as do we, brothers. Not a single one of you should miss the appointment with destiny in December. But heed me well, there are secret and disorganised forces working against us to prevent this glorious moment. But they will not prevail! As much as it grieves me, as a civilised man, it is my doleful obligation to pronounce a death sentence. Should the opportunity arise, understand me, I do not ask you to kill, but I do ask, nay, I *demand* of you as your bounden duty, to find and denounce the whereabouts of a degenerate named Jake Conley!"

Now I *did* screech!

The congregation turned as one to stare into the tree. I felt a hundred eyes searching to penetrate my camouflage in the foliage. At least one had succeeded because he pointed excitedly, indicating me to his companion. Others begged him to show them.

"Hark! Another sign! The Magus cried, "As before, the mere mention of the detestable name evokes outrage in our beloved familiar."

Is that what he's calling me, damn him! I'll tear out his eyes!

I took off from my branch and soared above the gathering. Flying low in a graceful circle over the oohing and aahing crowd, I don't know what came over me, I still can't explain it, instead of clawing at his face, I settled amicably like a mariner's parrot on his shoulder.

"Behold comrades! It is a sign!"

The fanatic gazed into my amber eyes and if I could have fulminated him with a glare there and then it would have saved a lot of trouble, but a death stare is one power I do not possess.

I remained for less than a minute, just enough time to study his facial features under the whitish paint. Why I hadn't ripped into it remains a mystery. I think it was wyrd or even weird! Back in the shelter of the foliage I listened carefully to the conversation of the dispersing audience. Most of it was banal about how I'd settled on the Magus and what an otherworldly omen that was. But I caught a female voice saying,

"I'll meet you later. I must speak to our leader about Jake Conley."

That interested me, so I waited until everyone except she and the Magus had gone. There was no need for me to fly nearer with my acute strigine hearing. Her words were quite clear.

"Master, it's about that Conley fellow. Is he such a danger?"

Although from my perch I didn't have a direct view of his facial reaction, his tone was impatient,

"I believe I said as much in my speech."

She gave an involuntary shudder, "I don't know if you recognise me, Magus, but I own the car rental business—"

That ruffled my feathers. I gave a reflex hoot as I remembered her voice.

In my shocked state I'd missed part of the conversation but catching up with her words, heard, "...he's using a different name on his licence but I recognised him from his book cover and from newspaper reports I'd seen."

"Good work. Does he have a car on hire at present?"

"Well no, but he tends to do one- or two-day rentals."

I saw him rest a hand on her shoulder, "Well done, my dear. It's late now but I'll give you a call in the morning and tell you what to do."

That should have been enough to warn me off hiring a car from her again, but, perversely, I didn't see it as a threat. In any case, I was more intent on following Sir Francis to locate his residence, for future reference. Flying above the churchyard, I watched him take leave of his follower and return to his car: a white Jaguar. He pulled smoothly away and I glided over the roofs and gardens of the outskirts of Pershore as he drove steadily to Cheltenham. That made perfect sense, as I knew he worked at GCHQ, whose unmistakable circular architecture now came into view. He continued past the precinct and through the western edge of town to take the Badgeworth road as far as the village. The car turned sharply into a driveway, where a white signboard standing like a sentinel advised Neighbourhood Watch, leading to an elegant Dutch-colonial-style house.

I settled in a tree, watched him park, enter the front door and saw a sequence of lights go on and off until he reached the master bedroom where he drew the curtains. I knew for sure now where Sir Francis Muir lived and was simultaneously impressed and baffled. Why do people who seem to have every luxury always want more? Within a quarter of an hour, I was back in my markedly inferior lodgings in Pershore, but it remained accommodation that offered me a warm, comfortable bed, which, once returned to human shape, was all I needed.

Sleepily, I reached for my mobile, almost vibrating itself off my bedside cabinet. I scowled at the digital time on the display but my frown disappeared when I saw who was calling.

"Alice!" I kept the irritation out of my voice but not the concern, "It's half-past two in the morning! Is everything all right?"

"Oh, Jake! I think I have a stalker; I was followed around Birmingham. I shook them off—"

"Hang on! First, you said a stalker, that is, *one*, then you said 'them'."

She calmed her voice with an effort, "Well, we're trained to shake off a tail, but they worked in relays." Explanation over, she returned to harassed mode, "I think there's a prowler in the grounds. I don't want to shoot him, Oh my God!"

"What!"

"No, nothing. Just the thought. What should I do?"

My mind had been racing to try to keep up with her and work out at the same time who was following her and why. The answer to both was quick in coming. It had to be the Brotherhood, who wanted to take her as a hostage to lure me out.

"Do you have a weapon, Alice?"

"Of course, regulation issue."

"Is it close to hand?"

"Yes."

"Good, now listen, barricade the door and be prepared to shoot to kill. I'm going to ring Sir Clive right away. He'll send in a squad to deal with any intruders. And I'll come over first thing in the morning."

My boss rang back at five o'clock to tell me that the emergency was over and that the police were holding two armed trespassers. Alice would now be provided with twenty-four-hour protection. Grateful, I updated him on the graveyard revelations and told him about my death sentence.

"Don't do anything foolish, dear boy! If in need, call this number."

"Thanks for everything, sir."

Despite his sound advice, I had an overwhelming desire to hold Alice in my arms. Still convinced the Porsche was too ostentatious, I returned to the car rental company. The owner, who also worked as receptionist and clerk—I think the low demand didn't justify employing others—greeted me with extreme politeness. Only on hearing her voice, did I recall her conversation with the Magus and, tardily, I became cautious.

"The car you had last time, Mr Rodgers, is out I'm afraid, but I have just the thing for you in Bay four." She flashed a key and gathered the paperwork. "We'll just look it over." She led me outside and walked around a silver Toyota, noting down a small scratch on the rear passenger side. Otherwise, the vehicle was blemish-free. As she signed the document, I glanced at the parked cars and among them noted the one I'd hired last time. Why had she lied? Alarm bells rang in my head, so I called her back and tossed her the keys.

"Do me a favour, would you? Just drive it out onto the road. I ran for cover around the side of the building. There was no explosion and she passed through the gateway and pulled over.

I hurried up to the car and came face to face with her.

She looked at me with a curious expression.

"I'm not sure I understand, Mr Rodgers."

"You can call me Jake. And I think *you'll* know I have to be extra careful."

Not waiting for a reply, I drove off only as far as the most convenient parking place. There, feeling paranoid, I checked the vehicle for any signs of interference. After all, a bomb could be on a timer. The only thing I lacked was a mirror on a stick to check under the chassis, but I was guessing that would-be assassins would have only had time to attach a magnetic device within easy reach, so I fumbled about in all the likely places and found nothing. Feeling melodramatic, I got back into the driving seat and turned on the ignition with nerves a-jangle but the vehicle didn't burst into flames.

I set off for Warwickshire and had gone twenty miles when the brakes began to feel spongy. At first, I dismissed it as imagination but when a refrigerator lorry in front started to brake erratically, I realised what was going on: I'd fallen into their trap. Twice, I came close to driving into the back of the white wall ahead of me and on the second occasion, the brakes hardly bit at all. Someone had cut through my brake fluid pipe and it had drained away. The next time the truck in front of me came to a sudden halt, I would plough into it and I doubted I'd come out of that alive. Thinking fast, I opened my driver's widow wide and concentrated hard. In seconds, I flew out up into the sky in the shape of a peregrine falcon. And not a moment too soon.

The hiss of air brakes, the scream of tyres and the crash of my car into the back of the lorry was followed by the crump of the explosion I had expected earlier. I circled over the scene of the 'accident' and watched the truck driver jump out of his cab and run to stare into the flaming vehicle. He couldn't get close to the inferno but withdrew hastily and waved at an oncoming van, pointlessly, as nobody could fail to see the orange flames and the column of black smoke pluming from the wreck. Now the killer was making a call, whether to report 'job done' or calling the emergency services I'll never know. Nor can I understand my reluctance to shape-shift. It's so much easier and quicker to fly to Warwickshire. Why rent a car when you can be a peregrine falcon? But then, my head is anything but straight!

I flew into our neat garden and after carefully ensuring the police watchmen didn't see me revert to being human, to their amazement, I opened our front door and walked in as bold as you like. They didn't like it one jot! Moments later, a flustered young officer rang the doorbell.

"Mr Conley, forgive me, sir, I have to ask how you passed our security cordon?"

I smiled at the puzzled face.

"You're doing an excellent job, sergeant. I'm afraid I can't tell you that—Official Secrets Act, I'm sure you understand." I winked at him, and to make him feel better, said, "But I can assure you, the people you have to keep out don't have access to that particular method."

Of that I was certain and he seemed satisfied; he tipped his cap and went back into position. Instead, I bounded upstairs and took Alice in my arms and rolled with her onto the bed. There were some things we had to catch up on, one of them being sleep after our disturbed night, but that came later. As did the television report showing the dreadful images of the mangled, burnt-out Toyota. *A rental car, taken out in the name of a thirty-nine-year-old tourist named James Rodgers...*

"That would be me, darling," I smiled at my wife. "It'll be a real conundrum for poor old forensics when they find no trace of human remains. Also, I wonder how the lorry driver explained away his emergency stop."

I had to tell her how I'd saved myself—no problem with Alice as she had already seen elves and knew about my various supernatural powers. A man and wife should have no secrets from each other. As I often tell her, "Behave yourself or I'll turn into a gorilla!" Not that I would, of course. In fact, I didn't feel like joking. I had gained time as the Brotherhood of the Wand would presume me dead if the police kept a strict reserve on the absence of a body. Regarding that, another call to Sir Clive was in order.

SEVENTEEN
PERSHORE, WORCESTERSHIRE, NOVEMBER 2022 AD

As ever, happy in my own company, I lay low knowing that the death sentence issued by the Brotherhood was in force and my whereabouts could be denounced at any moment. Although the days seemed endless left to myself, I used them to deliberate on a strategy to combat the imminent planned assault on Nature. For hours on end, I pondered in vain until, at the beginning of November, on a day when the sky couldn't decide whether it was white or pale grey, I had an idea. I glanced out of the window at the wind-driven rain thrashing against the pane and basked in the warmth of my room and the pleasure of emerging from mental paralysis.

Among the limited belongings I carry with me when away from home, lying beside my regulation issue Glock 17, was a statuette of the Anglo-Saxon goddess, Freya. It had been commissioned by my ex-wife Liffi and was a delightful piece of art sculpted by a Lincolnshire heathen named Kenneth Robinson. She didn't take it with her to Aelfheim, saying that she didn't need it there and it might be better in my custody. The same artist had created the totem still standing in Freya's temple in the Yorkshire Wolds. Now, the statuette was central to my plan. I took it lovingly from my case and placed it on the chest of drawers under the window.

I knew very well that Freya did and didn't exist. She was an angel, a seraph who had helped me overcome demonic forces in the affair of the Snape ring. The seraphim cannot present themselves before a person, otherwise, their awesome splendour would drive a human to insanity. That was why the granddaughter of Adam came to me in the guise of the beautiful goddess, Freya. She had endowed me with many of the powers I possessed such as shape-shifting. I knew that she held the best interests of mankind close to her heart and, indeed, God had raised her to a seraph because she had resisted the wiles of the Evil One. Now, more than ever, humanity needed her help—at least, the more vulnerable people did: the poor and the humble. But, I mused, not only mankind required help but also the planet itself.

I knelt in front of the statuette and began to pray to Freya with a strange mixture of heathen and Christian supplications. I was still about these devotions when my forehead hurt so much I almost lost consciousness. I placed my hand on the furniture to stop myself from keeling over and heard the sound of ruffling feathers—Freya! She had come, as usual wearing her cloak of falcon feathers.

"Goddess!" I cried.

"Jake Conley!" Her tone was severe, "You know you should not invoke my presence but from your prayer, I gather there is dire danger. Tell me about it."

Awestruck, I probably babbled incoherently, but it didn't matter because she could read the contents of my mind. I was still gabbling when she held up her hand, causing her exposed breast to rise tantalisingly. She smiled at my obvious desire and subsequent embarrassment.

"Hold!" she said, "You have told me everything, yes, in your thoughts. You did well to summon me. These dark forces must be stopped. You, who have studied the beliefs of your ancestors, know that there is a veil between Midgard—as Freya, she referred to the

Earth in Anglo-Saxon terms—and the other eight worlds. You have seen the flimsy fabric rent open recently. You also know that Ragnarök or what Christians call the Apocalypse will one day invest the planet. Abuse of the earth powers such as planned by this Brotherhood..." she pronounced the name without the slightest venom since her words exuded infinite calmness and wisdom, "...can hasten the onset and this does not affect just Midgard, unfortunately. The Midgard Serpent, the mythical Jormungand, once aroused will thrash around, rending the veil that separates Midgard from Aelfheim and menacing even the bridge to Asgard. This cannot be allowed to happen." She paused and frowned solemnly, her eye settling on the statuette. She raised a hand, palm outward, towards it and I watched it transform into a perfect replica of the goddess standing before me.

"That's better," she said, now use it to summon Liffi. "You are not alone, Jake Conley."

The air in the bedroom of my lodgings rippled and she vanished. I stared at the statuette, whose beautiful features seemed to smile at me. I felt an acute sense of loss and emptiness, but it was momentary. Seconds later, I recovered, knowing that I was not forsaken.

Once again, I knelt in front of the figurine, but this time, I didn't pray. Instead, I concentrated and said, "Liffi, you must come at once—the world is in danger!"

As before, the air in the bedroom oscillated, it parted like a curtain opening and into the room stepped a beautiful elfin creature.

"Liffi!" I leapt to my feet and made to embrace her, but the fierce flashing glare in her green eyes and her outstretched hand palm upward, stopped me in my tracks.

"Do not dare lay hands on the Queen of the Elves!"

"But Liffi, we were once man and wife."

"In another lifetime, Jake Conley. You have dared to summon me from the side of my husband and King. Speak! Lest something unspeakable happens to you," she threatened.

My mind was in turmoil. This was the woman who once loved

me and I, her. Now she seemed like an alluring, unattainable but cold and hostile marble statue.

I gazed at her with new eyes and began the long tale of earth powers and the Brotherhood of the Wand. I ended by explaining what Freya had advised me.

Liffi' expression had softened. A strange elfin smile brightened her beautiful face and stepping forward before I could react, her tongue was probing for mine. It was more than flesh and blood could endure: first the bare-breasted Freya and now the Elf Queen. She pushed me away, again the enigmatic smile flickered across and illuminated the lovely countenance.

"There, you deserved that, Jake Conley! The elves will work together with your forces to stop this insanity. I have seen the Midgard Serpent and it is a terrible sight. The White Goddess keeps it in check but if the balance is disturbed, there is no knowing what will be unleashed."

"I'm afraid there is, Liffi. Do you not remember, in the Red Horse Vale, you told me how we two, our wyrd, were predestined to fight together at Ragnarök?"

To my disappointment, she looked blank for a moment but then grinned,

"We had some adventures in Midgard, did we not? Life is far more serene in Aelfheim, Jake, and the elves live in synergy with nature—in perfect harmony, the opposite of here. You are right, we must fight side by side to stop this infamy. Just like old times, eh, Jake?"

He stepped forward. Again, the flashing eyes.

"You really must learn your place, my friend, and treat me like royalty."

Her eyes settled on the statuette of Freya.

"You still have that. But it seems somehow different, more beautiful," she hesitated, "...more realistic."

I was still smarting from her words but didn't want to be petty.

"You're right, Freya was here a few minutes ago and, maybe she didn't appreciate the likeness. Anyhow, she changed it."

"Ah, was she here? Well then, I must go. Avebury, December 21st. There is much to prepare."

She raised her arms, spread her hands wide and a portal appeared. Liffi stepped into it and her voice drifted back as she vanished. I caught a glimpse of a serene sunrise that contrasted with the filthy weather outdoors and heard, "until the solstice, take care, Jake."

Gone. Emptiness. Alone, once more, I sat heavily and disconsolate on the bed. Liffi didn't love me anymore. But that was as it should be and I loved Alice. Ah, Alice! I couldn't call her, in case my mobile was bugged. But how I wanted to hear her comforting voice in that moment of disconsolation.

I must have remained there brooding for a good ten minutes about my two encounters. I'll confess to more than a little sexual frustration, but what red-blooded man wouldn't have been the same? What other motive could there have been for my momentary lapse of reason?

To hell with it! I'm calling Alice!

And that is what I did. We were on the phone for at least ten minutes. It was long enough for her to cheer me up and to wish that the distance between us didn't exist. Still, she was more sensible than me and obeying protocol to the letter. She knew how to lay low and keep out of harm's way.

Th call over, I went back to planning. To my surprise, I was interrupted by my landlady knocking at the door.

"Mr Rodgers? There's a gentleman asking for you. I let him into the guest lounge."

"Thank you, Mrs Woolstencroft, I'll be right down."

Nobody knew my alias except the car rental woman, which meant the Brotherhood! I let her go and listened for her step on the stairs before grabbing the Glock and tucking it into my belt behind my back and under my sweater. With just enough time to rue my call to Alice, I left the bedroom and went downstairs. If GCHQ didn't have the technology to tap a mobile, nobody in the UK had. The door to the guest lounge was closed and I could hear my landlady pottering about with pans in the kitchen, so no witness saw me pull out the gun before I opened the door.

I levelled the weapon at the man standing in front of the fireplace whose hand was straying inside his jacket.

"You can take the pistol out slowly and lay it at your feet. Then kick it towards me. Don't think I'll hesitate to use this."

Wisely, he obeyed to the letter.

"Now turn around and face the fire."

As he did this, I picked up his gun. I don't fancy myself as a James Bond; in fact, I don't want to be an agent at all, but somehow, I found the courage and, in the manner of film spies, I hit him with all my might with his pistol—a metallic rabbit punch. His knees buckled and I caught him to lower him noiselessly to the carpet. It's the first time I've knocked a man out and whilst I was surprised at my efficiency, my mind was racing. Mrs Woolstencroft mustn't find me in this compromising situation. I needed time but there was an unconscious man in front of the fire. I looked around the small room. Only one possibility remained, to drag him behind the sofa. He was as heavy as I feared, but I'd hit him well and he didn't stir. That was an advantage, but he was a dead weight. Nonetheless, I managed and after much heaving and carpet rucking, I got him into position before readjusting the settee and the rug. From the door, there was no sign of his prone figure. The room appeared empty, so I could vacate it calmly. In the hall, at the foot of the stairs, I smelt the delicious aroma of cooking food and the out of tune singing of the woman.

I bounded upstairs, grabbed my coat and belongings, put my training to use as I left the property with the utmost stealth, ensuring there was no accomplice or other surveillance. I took back streets until I was forced to stride along the main road to the Parks. There, I retrieved my Porsche, settled the bill and was on my way to Warwickshire in minutes. There, I would enjoy the benefits of

Alice's police protection. Poor Mrs Woolstencroft, I hoped the intruder would leave without frightening her. I'd paid my rent in advance, so she wasn't out of pocket.

The Brotherhood of the Wand was becoming a nuisance. With the solstice just over a month away, they were sure to redouble their efforts to neutralise me. They didn't know that I could call on the British armed forces, the elves and my ingenuity. My only doubts for the moment were about the latter. I urgently needed a workable plan for 21st December.

The idea of being in a cosily protected environment soon vanished. I'd been back with Alice little more than four hours when a knock came at the door. It was the same young sergeant I had spoken with before.

"Sir, just to let you know that we're away now. Orders from above, I'm afraid."

"That's it? Just like that? Who gave these instructions?"

He looked embarrassed and could see that I was unhappy.

"Came through on the radio, sir. Ours is not to reason why—"

"Yes, I know. Thanks anyway, have a good day."

He tipped his cap and walked down the garden path.

There was little doubt that the Brotherhood was behind this. I picked up my mobile to ring Sir Clive, stared at it and changed my mind.

"Darling, may I use your phone? There's a trace on mine."

Perfect enunciation from the other end, complete with affectation, I'd recognise my boss's voice anywhere.

"Alice, my dear gell! How are you?"

"Sorry, sir, it's Jake. My mobile has been compromised."

I told him what had happened at my lodgings and now, about the removal of protection.

"Well, I don't think you killed the fellow. I'd have heard by now. But this surveillance withdrawal...bad business. Leave it with me."

A few minutes later, he rang back.

"This has Frankie Muir's pawprints all over it. The order came from GCHQ. He always was a sneaky little wretch at school. Well, look, I'll send a car round with a couple of our best men. You and your lady wife pack some necessities and we'll ship you off to a safe house, dear boy. Oh, by the way, I want a written report on Frankie's shenanigans. You can dispatch it with one of the boys when his relief comes through, all right?"

Frankie, is it? Old school chums, he must know Sir Francis Muir very well.

Of course, it was all right, I needed Sir Clive to be fully on board. The way things were shaping, we required all the protection MI5 could provide.

The vehicle that pulled up outside our gate was a black Jeep with darkened windows. Every time I saw a car of that make, my mind went back to when I'd had my accident and my brain had changed forever. By association, I wondered if my psychic gifts would be strong enough to thwart the massed forces of the Brotherhood—time would tell, but now the moment had arrived to follow our minders.

EIGHTEEN

RURAL WARWICKSHIRE, NOVEMBER 2022 AD

ALICE WORKED ON HIGH-DEFINITION PHOTOGRAPHS OF manuscripts whilst at home, meaning that our confinement in a safe house didn't affect her work. As for me, I passed the time trying to conceive a scheme to deal with the Brotherhood. Aware that the next new moon was only five weeks away and that I'd had no contact with the strategic forces that would be required to prevent the onset of catastrophe, I thrashed around for a solution.

Frustration at being penned inside a property probably less than twenty miles from home, combined with anxiety, left me more introspective than usual. In a deeply reflective moment, I questioned my abilities. Everyone else rated them so highly but I felt inadequate in the face of the task awaiting us. Why should it be so?

I thought about the limitations holding me back. Any other man in the world blessed with the power to shift shape would be using it continually. Without rational explanation, I used it as sparingly as an ophthalmic surgeon dispenses medicine from an eyedropper. Without bothering to analyse my reluctance, I recognised that my attitude was jeopardising the futures of others.

Decision taken, I walked through to disturb Alice, poring over

Anglo-Saxon calligraphy. She was trying to make sense of fragments of a poem, but I needed to tell her that I was about to fly out of the window as my absence would be noted.

"Sorry to interrupt, but I need to reconnoitre Salisbury Plain. It's going to take a military operation to stop the Brotherhood of the Wand. So, I'm going to transform into a falcon and do aerial surveillance of the area. I'll be back before nightfall. I know it's cold outside, but I'll need you to open the bedroom window wide before it gets dark. You'd better give me ten minutes now and then close it."

Alice looked excited. She had never seen me change shape.

"Can I come and watch you become a falcon?"

I am full of all sorts of complexes, most of which I put down to the after-effects of my road accident. A protective instinct made me refuse over-brusquely and I felt I had to explain.

"The peregrine is a beautiful creature, Alice, but still, it's a bird. It would be traumatising for you to see your husband transform into a raptor." I tried to jolly away the offended expression clouding her face. "I'm already *fowl* enough in your eyes! Bye, darling." I took her in my arms and instead of pliant warm lips was met with a cold hard kiss, which left me feeling hurt.

I closed the bedroom door so that she wouldn't see the transformation, convinced it was for the best, and flew out into the buffeting wind, exulting in the freedom of flight. The minders far below couldn't possibly conceive of how I had flown the coop!

Orienting myself only using manmade features, like road signs, since there was no trace of the sun in the November sky, I remembered the wonderful short poem *November* by Thomas Hood and recited it from memory:

> **No shade, no shine, no butterflies, no bees,**
> **No fruits, no flowers, no leaves, no birds! —**
> **November!**
> No birds! Well, there is one notable exception!

Even as I thought this, the wind swept me hundreds of yards off course, but it was so exhilarating that I didn't care. Only when I realised that I had no idea where I was, did I begin to panic. Even a falcon gets tired combatting contrary currents. I found a sorry-looking oak bereft of leaves and settled on a bough close to its trunk to gain respite from the leonine wind. November can rarely be described as charming. If anything, its attraction lies in the beauty of austerity. There are people who, attracted to anti-aesthetics, adore greyness. I'm not one of them. I prefer a sunny, flower-laden May any time.

Not that I had a compass tucked away in my feathers, but it turned out later that a cold north-easterly was chilling my countrymen. This was beneficial to my journey. Energy recovered after my break, I waited, like a helicopter pilot in a gale, for a lull to get airborne once more. It came and with a few strong beats of my wings, soon I was high over a motorway. In this part of the country, it had to be the M5 and in that case, before long, with the driving wind behind me, I should see the River Severn. The choppy water of the great river challenged the sky in the matter of greyness. But I was happy to see it because my knowledge of local geography was good and Avebury would now be only fifty miles to the south-east as the hawk flies.

Over Salisbury Plain, I began to have military thoughts. Below me were the monuments: the unmistakable mound of Silbury Hill, Windmill Hill, Avebury henge, Stonehenge and the various barrows and processional routes. How marvellous to see them from on high. Now I concentrated on the earth currents and was relieved to see the pattern of silver ribbons clearly in my mind—so much for snide comments about *bird brain!* I suspected that I could see them better and with more understanding than I would in human form. Logically, as a falcon, my instinctive powers were nearer to Mother Nature.

My eye was taken at once by Knoll Down, where old, gnarled trees stood on what was once an earthwork of considerable size. I noted the wide entrance and my gaze followed a path leading along its length. At the far end, it narrowed and the path split, as did the earth energy, which was flowing across the entire earthwork from a place where two smaller currents merged to form a serpent at Beckhampton. Each current issued from a spiral that from up here looked like a ram's horn because one was clockwise and the other, the opposite. I recognised them as Michael and Mary energy vortices joining together to form the Serpent's Tail. This valuable insight provided me with a campaign plan. I would need to share my idea with the generals, of course. The Mary spiral was at the edge of a farmer's field. The Michael force ran outside the trees of the earthwork. My eye switched to Silbury, which was away to the southeast—a perfect communications centre. From there, if it came to it, both extremities of the serpent's body would be visible at the crucial time. I flew over the sacred landscape, gaining an intimate and awe-inspiring knowledge, before winging away, satisfied, to fly into the teeth of the wind on my return. I'm no ornithologist but I imagine my fellow peregrines do not venture out in such energy-sapping conditions. My relief at seeing the bedroom window open was surpassed only by, once back in human form, closing it before flopping exhausted onto the bed.

I awoke to Alice gently stroking my hair back from my forehead.

"What time is it?" I murmured in a daze.

"Not late, about half-past eight. Now, tell me, what have you been up to?"

I countered with a question.

"Did our heavies miss me?"

"I don't think they noticed you'd gone. One of them came in to check on me and asked after you. I told him you were having a lie-down and not to disturb you. It might be a good idea to show yourself downstairs, aren't you hungry?"

My stomach rumbled in confirmation. In any case, I needed to verify their relief schedule as I wanted to transmit the plan I now related to Alice before we went to the kitchen. Sir Clive would be most interested and if I judged his reaction aright to be as I hoped, he would immediately trigger the necessary arrangements.

Two days later, the changeover took place and one of the relieved men took my sealed envelope for delivery to Sir Clive Cochrane in the Ministry. The day after, Alice's phone rang and our boss asked her to pass me. Not calling on my mobile was a sensible precaution and Sir Clive was taking no risks.

"Now, dear boy, we can't talk freely." I think he was implying the possibility of my wife's phone being tapped too. "I'll just say that the recipe you sent me was delicious and my guests enjoyed it. I shall most certainly have our cooks prepare it next month."

After this brief call ended, I explained it to Alice.

"Sir Clive approves of the plan and he's spoken to the Chiefs of Staff who will go along with it. They'll be ready to carry it out on 21st December."

"So, everything's under control," she smiled, but I could see something was troubling her.

I poured us each a glass of whisky and as we relaxed basking in its warming glow, I asked,

"What's bothering you, my love?"

She frowned, pursed her lips and hesitated,

"Maybe I'm exaggerating, but I can't help but think that an organisation headed by some of the most powerful men in the country, located in GCHQ and with so much riding on their success, will just stand by and let your intervention thwart them." She paused, swirled the liquid in her glass and darted a glance to see my reaction. Reassured that I was considering her words carefully, she continued, "With the detection technology at their disposal, there's every possibility that Sir Clive's meeting with the military has been infiltrated either by human or technological means."

"Are you saying that they'll already know our plan and will stop at nothing to derail it?"

"I also think it's quite likely that they'll move against us before the December date. We think we're secure here but just think about it. These people have access to the most secret material in Britain. They'll know where every safe house is located and the weaknesses of each one. They can track any phone by its number and they'll already know Sir Clive called here. Luckily, he's an expert and kept the call short. We have to hope that they didn't pinpoint it but it's odds on that they had time enough to narrow it to a rough geographical area, which in turn, makes their task easier to identify which safe house we're in."

For a woman of few words like Alice, that was a long speech and it revealed how frightened of the Brotherhood she had become.

I'd already had some of these fears at the back of my mind, but to hear them expressed so cogently, convinced me of the need to react. We couldn't afford to freeze like terrified rabbits caught in the oncoming headlights. My wife was too bright to be fobbed off with comforting words. I knew she'd prefer me to share her concerns.

"When we're located, they'll send a squad to eliminate us. So, we have to move first."

Breath rushed through her nostrils, and relieved, she said,

"By moving first, do you mean taking Sir Francis Muir out of the equation? Jake, you can't just walk into GCHQ. You'd be arrested as soon as security checked your name."

"I'm not thinking of doing that, Alice. You're forgetting that I know where the Magus lives. His house will have a high-tech alarm system but I can get past anything. Once I get him alone, I'll be able to ruin all his plans."

"Tomorrow's already 2 December, there's not much time left—"

"Did you think I'd forgotten? It *is* my birthday, after all! The fact is, I don't feel very festive."

"Well, we'll see. I'm going down to the kitchen to bake you a cake."

She'd only been gone a moment when I heard her scream my name.

I rushed to the stairs and flung myself sideways as a bullet thumped into the landing wall. The shot had been suppressed, maybe that was why I hadn't detected anything before.

Alice! Oh my God! They'd better not have harmed her.

I heard footsteps on the stairs. No matter how stealthily an intruder came up, the risers had been constructed to creak a warning. I realised with a sinking feeling that I was without a gun in the bedroom. If ever there was a time to shift shape, it was now. But there was not enough room for a falcon to manoeuvre effectively.

Come on, Jake, think dammit!

Then I had an awesome idea! Concentrating fiercely, I transformed myself and slithered up the side of the wardrobe and waited on top, ready to strike. The neurotoxins in the venom of a black mamba paralyse the victim who, without antidotal treatment later dies. I had chosen to transform into the fastest snake on earth. The door flew open and a man entered, holding a gun fitted with a suppressor ahead of him with both hands in orthodox style as his eyes searched the room. He peered under the bed, grunted, and turned to inspect inside the wardrobe. He didn't see me coming. A lightning strike and my fangs were in his neck, injecting deadly venom. His weapon fell to the carpet and he collapsed, incapable of movement. I slithered away from him, back up the wardrobe and coiled ready to react again if needed. The thought of changing back into human form and gathering his firearm hadn't appealed to me because again I'd heard the stairs creak and feared I'd be caught reaching for the gun.

This decision was vindicated immediately when a lowered voice hissed, "Ralph, are you in there? Ralph?" With exceeding caution, the second gunman entered, armed just as his comrade. His attention was taken by the prone figure on the floor. Sure, he looked around the room but didn't notice my dark form in the shadow above the wardrobe. Now he bent to take the pulse in the man's neck but withdrew his fingers with a gasp when he saw the puncture marks of my bite. Too late for him to react, I sprang down from the wardrobe and he only had time to squirm and shriek before my fangs sank into his flesh. His knees buckled and he crashed to lie over the body of his fellow intruder.

The irony of all this is that I have a phobia about snakes, even innocuous ones. Even when they are safely behind armoured glass in a reptile house, I can hardly bear to look at them. Happily, I couldn't see myself in a mirror. I listened carefully before I changed back into my own body and picked up a 9mm Smith and Wesson with its attached silencer.

Alice!

Those damned stairs creaked for householder and intruder alike. Anyone in the lounge would hear my arrival but they could not know whether I was a friend or a target. Alice saved me. She was sitting, cuffed to a chair and gagged with a strip of duct tape. As I entered the room, her eyes frantically signalled to her left. I dived to the floor in the same instant and heard the dull crump of the shot. At the same time, I identified the figure, the barrel of his gun changing the direction to point at me. Once again, my fast reactions paid off as my bullet knocked him off his feet and his discharge planted a projectile harmlessly into the ceiling. I'm not a trained shot like Alice and other agents but my few attempts on the range when accompanying my wife were always respectable. I leapt to my feet and yelled,

"Are there any more of them?"

Alice shook her head and I hurried over to my victim. One glance was enough. I hardly believed that my shooting ability was so lethal. The bullet had hit him in the chest and must have pierced an artery because he was beyond human aid. I retrieved a small key from his hip pocket.

Crossing the room to Alice. I gently peeled away the tape from her face. She ran her tongue over her lips and spat.

"There were three of them," she said anxiously.

"No longer," I said cryptically, unfastening her handcuff.

"You mean, you dealt with them too? Oh, Jake!"

I looked around the room,

"What about our men?"

Her eyes searched around and she went to the window and recoiled.

"You'd better look!"

I stepped over and saw the figure lying on the patio like a broken doll.

"Quickly! Let's check on him."

I bent over our guard and felt for a pulse. Thankfully, it was there, weak, but perceptible.

"Phone for an ambulance, he's lost too much blood. I think he's been hit in the abdomen. Get the police too, Alice. There's plenty of tidying up to be done here."

How the devil am I going to explain the snake bites?

The most urgent thing was to find our other security man. I began a thorough search of the premises, whilst Alice peeled back the clothing of the wounded man and used her training to put a temporary dressing in place.

The second man was lying unconscious in a storeroom, where he'd been thrown by his assailants. A splash of cold water and a damp cloth to his head soon had him groaning and his eyelids flickering. I fetched him a glass of water and explained the situation to him, carefully avoiding any mention of a black mamba.

After the police arrived, I used my mobile to ring Sir Clive. Our cover had been compromised, so there was no need to avoid using my phone. I put him in the picture and asked him to clamp down on the two inexplicable deaths.

"No problem, there, old boy, we can shut down anything when national security is involved. How did they die, by the way?"

"I'll write it in my report, sir. I think it's better to say nothing on the phone."

"Yes, quite right. Well, leave it to me—and jolly good work, dear boy!"

Sir Clive might be pleased but I was fuming. Lucky for the

Magus that Alice had been unhurt. My loathing of his plans for our country and its people was now underpinned by personal hatred. The time had come to settle scores with Sir Francis Muir once and for all.

NINETEEN

BADGEWORTH, GLOUCESTERSHIRE, DECEMBER 2022 AD

A SMALL INTERMITTENT RED LED LIGHT MOUNTED IN A plastic box blinked a warning to any intruder that the mansion was protected by an alarm system. It was probably linked to the local police station. I had overcome the perimeter fencing without difficulty on my falcon wings. My problem now was entry without forcing the door or windows of the Magus's house. I prowled around the large building, my eyes alert for CCTV cameras and managed not to be filmed. Just as I began to despair of ever gaining access, I spotted the only sign of poor maintenance—a crack in the mortar next to an architrave of the rear entrance. I contemplated and decided it was just wide enough for a small rodent to squeeze through: maybe a shrew.

My hesitation was due to not knowing whether Sir Francis Muir was a cat lover. What a disaster to end up in feline claws to be tormented before death. But what was I thinking? If such a creature appeared, I would transform into a tiger and send the mouser mewling away. Courage regained, I concentrated, transformed into a field mouse and scurried to squeeze my elastic bones through the dirty, dusty crevice and emerge into a spotless kitchen with a reassuring absence of animal food bowl.

Back into my human shape, I used a small flashlight to move around and when its beam struck a bottle of twenty-three-year-old Teaninch, I poured myself a good measure of the single malt and settled in an armchair to enjoy Frankie's tipple. The baronet treated himself well, I noted the label declared it to be a Limited Edition and classified it as a Rare Malt. I switched off my flashlight and sat back in the gloom to appreciate the light peaty taste, and rolled it around my palate enjoying the sensation of smoke and oak and the long, mellow finish. This was one to add to my list.

The owner of this mansion delighted in luxury, the lounge was as neat and tidy as the kitchen. Surely, Sir Francis employed an excellent housekeeper. The thought that there might be someone else in the building hadn't occurred to me but a home of that size would require staff: cleaners, cook, maybe even a secretary. But at the moment it was as quiet as the Pershore Abbey graveyard. Also, I was savouring the owner's whisky too much to reconnoitre the interior. Sighing contentedly, I settled back to consider what I had to do. I had never killed a man in cold blood, previously I had been forced to react to save my life or that of a loved one. This was different. For the first time, I was motivated on the one hand, by hate and on the other, by a love of my fellow man, who must be saved from a monster thinking only of personal power and gain.

The whisky gave me the courage to confront my possibilities, but also, strangely, brought lucidity to my reasoning. After all, there was a workable alternative to killing the wretch. Among my gifts, I had the means of binding men's minds to my will as I had done with Sir Thomas Etherington, Chief Executive Officer of Envogas, one of the most important fracking companies in the UK, back in my days in the Red Horse Vale, when I put an end to extraction there. Reducing Sir Francis Muir to subservience would be infinitely preferable to a cold-blooded killing. As they say, the end does not justify the means, not when one's immortal soul is at stake.

I had no scruples though as I stole another glass of the exquisite whisky and I was appreciating it when I heard the crunch of tyres on gravel. He was home! I merely settled back in the armchair and waited. Within minutes, Sir Francis Muir would become my lapdog, an obedient servant to my every whim.

Footsteps approached and I half-closed my eyes as bright light replaced the gloom of the lounge.

"Well, well! The effrontery of it! You break into my home and sit helping yourself to my prized whisky! And how do you suppose you are going to leave here alive, Mr Conley?"

I concentrated on binding his mind to subservience but he just stood there grinning.

"Ah, a very good try, but it won't work with me, young fellow! You are confronting one of the most expert—if not *the* most formidable— shamans in the world.

Dammit! It's not working, I'll change into a black mamba again.

He sneered, read my mind, and his voice mocking said, "There's no use changing into a snake, I'd simply become a mongoose and tear you apart. Then you'd transform into a jackal to kill the mongoose and I'd—"

"I don't care," I said, taking a gun from my jacket pocket and levelling it at him. I swear I would have killed him there and then but the butt of the pistol became searingly hot and I released my grip with a howl and let it fall to the carpet.

"You see," he smirked, "I'm far more adept at the dark arts than you'll ever be! I think you can dismiss all ideas of ever leaving these premises alive, Mr Conley. How dare you suppose that you could obstruct the most important historic event in the history of mankind?"

His eyes bored into mine and I felt my will to resist draining away, but I would not submit so easily and concentrated as fiercely as I could.

Locked in a mental conflict like two wrestlers staggering around a ring, at last, he stopped and looked at me with renewed respect.

"Perhaps I have underestimated you. All the more reason for you not to escape with your life." He pulled out a mobile phone and I swooped for the gun.

"I wouldn't use that phone if I were you."

His lip curled in contempt,

"Ow!" I cried and dropped the weapon again, shaking my hand to ease the pain caused by the blistering heat.

"My goodness, you are a slow learner!"

I flung myself at him to wrest the mobile from his hand. We finished rolling on the floor as he tried to reach the phone, presumably to call in his heavies. He struck me a stunning blow to the side of the head, but I managed to get a hold on his throat and began throttling him. Somehow, he raised a knee sharply into my midriff and forced me to release my grip. I fell backwards and he sprang for my gun which I kicked out of reach. Pouncing, he was on me again and raining blows to my head. Most of them I blocked with my arms, but surely, younger than my opponent by twenty years, I would prevail. Sir Francis Muir had kept his physique lithe and well-honed, a credit to his lifestyle, so my task was far harder than mere age might suggest. We fought in the centre of the lounge both physically and mentally because when I decided to shift shape, he blocked me. I also sensed and thwarted his attempts at magic. How long we might have struggled to overcome each other I do not know, because something extraordinary happened.

Suddenly my opponent lay helpless, his body motionless entrapped in golden chains. This took me as much by surprise as it did him. His stillness after the fierce struggling was my first realisation that something had occurred. The second was his string of oaths followed by,

"Accursed elfin magic! How did you manage that, Conley?"

Of course, I had done nothing and looked wildly around the room but saw nothing and no one. I expected to see Liffi or one or more of her elves but we two were the only people in the room. I bent to pick up the gun and moved across to fire it at point-blank range.

My hand shook a little but I calmed myself and squeezed the trigger —nothing!

Has the devil blocked the pistol?

"I assure you, I have not!" he seemed unable to address me without sneering. "There are greater powers at work here, Conley!"

I checked the weapon, releasing and replacing the clip. There seemed nothing wrong with it, so I tried to shoot him again, but the pistol wouldn't fire. I hurried into the kitchen and removed a carving knife from a wooden block. I intended to slit his throat, but as I raised the sharp blade to perform the dreadful deed, the solid Sheffield steel curved, flaccid like a piece of artwork by Salvador Dali. I flung the useless object to the carpet.

"How the hell did you..."

I stopped, looked at his baffled face and gave up. It appeared he was protected and his death was not ordained.

I picked up his mobile and pocketed it.

"I'm going to leave you there to starve or die of thirst, you bastard!"

I walked over to the almost full bottle of whisky and took it.

"You won't be needing this where you're going—straight to Hell."

I grinned down at him, felt in his jacket pocket and removed his car keys.

"And you won't require your Mercedes, so I'll relieve you of it for my return journey. Now, I'm going to switch off the light and leave you to settle down for the night. May the Devil take you!"

I'm ashamed to say that I couldn't resist kicking his head as I strode past. It's never a good thing to strike a defenceless man, even if he is a fiend. To be fair to myself, I had many reasons to hate him and I ran through them in my mind as I travelled back to collect Alice. Most of the journey, though, I spent pondering the golden chains imprisoning the Magus. Surely, he was right when he spat out: *elfin magic*. It could only be the work of the *Ljósálfar*—the light elves. But was it they who had prevented me from using the gun and completing my task? Somehow, I thought not. It must have been an unseen diabolical entity. I regretted leaving the mansion without executing the Magus. The world was still at risk. I'd been lucky. I'd had no idea of who I was pitted against. I knew him to be evil and a conduit for Earth forces, but had been ignorant of his possession of shamanic powers and that cluelessness might have proved fatal.

Later, holding Alice in my arms, I was still shaken by the events in Badgeworth. With her usual intuition, my wife said,

"Oh Jake, you must have had a terrible time. Are you going to share that whisky with me?"

She knew that a companionable drink would be the best cure for my shattered nerves. She was also wise enough to let me recover before breaking her news.

"Liffi was here. She's so beautiful! Why on earth did you let her go, Jake?"

I almost dropped the priceless amber liquid,

"Liffi here? What are you saying?"

She studied my reactions to gauge whether I still had feelings for my former lover. Of course, I did, but not as she understood.

"She came to warn you about the Magus and his powers. The elves have been keeping an eye on him since you summoned her in November."

"She might have come earlier because forewarned is forearmed. As it is, her tardiness nearly cost me my life. It was elfin magic that saved me. But hang on! If Liffi was here, she can't have bound the Magus in chains."

"I think it was her husband, the king. Didn't you see him?"

"He must have wanted to remain invisible. But I wonder—" The inability to fire the gun still tormented me. Equally, what happened to the carving knife left me perplexed. I told Alice about these episodes.

She stared open-eyed and said, "And you're sure he wasn't using his superpowers?"

"He denied it and looked confused. I think there was some other invisible element in that room. And you know what that means."

"No."

"That he will be released and not starve to death. I'm afraid we're back to square one. What's more, he'll have a trace on his Mercedes—I saw the little red light glowing. We have to get out of here!"

"We can leave his car and take the Jeep. Bryan can drive." She was referring to the unharmed security man. "Let's go home, Jake. We'll be as safe there as anywhere.

I doubted that, but home appealed more than elsewhere. I wasn't afraid of a direct clash with the Magus because I'd held my own against him. The worrying thought was how many adherents he might muster for another attempt on my life.

TWENTY
WARWICKSHIRE, DECEMBER 2022 AD

Alice sat on the edge of the bed holding my hand and watching me burning up with fever. The doctor had just left the house, shaking his head and taking with him a blood sample for virological analysis. She had found my temperature running at 40.5°C, dangerously high, but I wasn't going to let them take me anywhere.

"Alice," I croaked.

"Sweetheart?"

I squeezed her hand and hoped she wouldn't argue.

"This is Frankie Muir's handiwork. Black magic! Listen, I want you to go to the shops. Find a black candle and a small rectangular mirror." Speaking was a struggle until she helped me sip from a glass of water. Refreshed, I added, "Oh, and while you're at it, buy a pack of sea salt." My voice had sunk to a whisper, "Is there any sage in the garden?"

I knew there was, of course, because Alice grew every kind of culinary herb for her delicious cooking. When she returned, carrying these acquisitions, I instructed her to place the mirror in the far corner of the room on the floor, with the black candle in front of it.

"Don't look in the mirror—ever—" I insisted, "now, light the taper."

"Would you mind telling me what's going on?"

I felt a shiver run up my spine and curled tighter into a foetal position. I couldn't prevent a groan.

"Jake!" My wife hurried away from the candle, now burning brightly, and dabbed my forehead with a cool damp cloth.

"Black absorbs negative energy and the mirror will reflect it to where it came from. Get the salt and sprinkle it in front of the bedroom door. Use it all, Alice, you can vacuum it up when I'm better. "Do you have a bundle of dried sage? Or do you only have the fresh leaves?"

"Both, why?"

"Bring them up here when you've done the salt."

Alice reappeared after several minutes and said,

"What's this about?"

"I want you to set the dried bundle alight and waft it around the room."

She gave me a hard stare, but Alice has faith in my psychic powers. Within moments, a pleasant woody aroma pervaded the room.

I was already feeling better and managed to explain.

"The ancient Greeks did this to release the plant spirit and revitalise the energy in the space concerned. It banishes conflict in the environment and relieves stress and illness, brings clarity and sharpens intuition. Nowadays, scientists have discovered that its smoke kills more than ninety per cent of airborne bacteria in a room."

"That's amazing! Is there anything else you need?"

"The fresh leaves."

I took them, crumpled them and pushed them under my pillow, retaining one and putting it on the tip of my tongue. My physical defences were raised as high as I could manage. So, I concentrated on my spiritual shield and began to pray and recite a mantra I'd devised years ago: a paean to Freya, who I had discovered to be an angel.

Muir's dark energy must have been extremely strong since it took over an hour for my temperature to drop to the normality of 37°C. But then, I felt almost sprightly, better than before my *illness*. Knowing that I had channelled the mischief and harm back whence it had come, cheered me. Downstairs, in my armchair, I began to fantasise that the strength of the malice might have been too strong for one man to emanate. Had Muir conducted a Black Mass, perhaps with a group of Templars? A voice from the kitchen door broke through my reverie,

"What are you doing out of bed?"

"I'm alright. Look! I jumped up and played the clown by bounding around the room."

"Well, thank goodness. You had me worried. That fever was worthy of a shire horse, never mind a little weed, like you!"

"This little weed is going to bring Francis Muir down, I swear it! He's a master of the Dark Arts, I'll give him that. Better leave the candle and the salt overnight. And don't look in the mirror whatever you do."

Settling back into my favourite armchair, my intuition sharpened by the burnt sage, I began to meditate. Respect for my foe, mixed with a healthy dose of fear helped as much as the sage. I pondered the spiritual outcome of my struggle and realised that patience and persistence, nothing else, would serve to bring the rewards I sought. But my problem was how best to do what was necessary to circumvent the menace looming before the solstice?

I was certain that only by directing my full attention to it would I accomplish my task. The situation momentarily was all in Muir's favour unless, somehow, I could harness positive energies to direct the outcome as I wished. One thing I have learnt to my advantage is that looking back with regret or gazing forward pointlessly robs myself of a present opportunity. Old thoughts and patterns of behaviour negate the chance to advance. And advance I would—on Sir Francis Muir, the Magus.

I had an idea I couldn't shake off, but to achieve the plan would require considerable help from Sir Clive Cochrane. I travelled across to London, preferring to speak with him face to face.

"I need to walk into GCHQ with the absolute trust of Sir Francis Muir."

"My dear boy! I should have you certified. How do you suppose you can do that?"

"Can you not create some important role for me, indispensable to him?"

"And even if I did, don't you imagine he'd have you arrested as soon as he saw your face, old chap?"

"That's not a problem because he'll be looking at an attractive young Irishwoman."

Sir Clive gaped at me. I'm sure he felt in urgent need of a straightjacket and a sedative. The former for me.

"*Irish*woman?"

I chortled, "You forget, sir, I grew up in Tullamore and can command my old brogue whenever it suits. I'm a descendant of the O'Conghalaigh family of County Offaly."

"*Bejabbers!*" he joked, "Very well, Irish...but *woman?*"

"You also fail to remember, sir, that I can transform, I mean, shape-shift. I think a pretty auburn-haired *colleen* is called for. I'll need a new identity, passport, what-have-you, but I'm sure you can see to that."

The sardonic expression that he reserved, I believe exclusively for me, curled his lip. "Very well, Jayne Ryan, bring me four regulation photographs with your new face, tomorrow. You were born in Carrigaholt, County Clare." He jotted it down in his black notebook. "Mouth of the Shannon, on the coast, all right? Father's a greenkeeper at the East Clare Golf Club, named Arthur and your mother is Mary. You were born on September 28, 1990. I'll see you tomorrow." It turned out the old fox knew the Ryans and had played the course over the years.

There were technical problems to overcome and the first was clothing. I could hardly wander into a boutique as a man and leave as a woman. To get around this, I went to a fashionable clothes store and took advice from a very helpful assistant, who was pleased to select garments best suited to an auburn-haired *wife* that I invented. Well, not entirely fabricated, because I used Alice's measurements for shoes and underwear. I also visited the cosmetics department of a store and bought products suitable for my complexion, assuring the heavily made-up and sceptical young woman that my wife's skin tone was the same as mine.

I booked into a hotel, locked the bedroom door, undressed, had a shower and then concentrated on shape-shifting. I had to imagine the precise weight, height, hair, and physical features of my ideal woman. This called for considerable mental effort, much more than any other transformation I had previously undertaken. The full-length mirror on the wardrobe door reflected my astonished expression. My new persona was extraordinarily beautiful, setting aside the fact that a splendid naked thirty-two-year-old redhead was gazing back at me, someone accustomed to admiring the charms of the opposite sex, I had to admit that I'd created a real head-turner.

The question now was whether I'd cope with the technical difficulties other women had overcome as teenagers. Watching me tie back my long, wavy hair with an elastic band would have had Alice in stitches, but after several attempts, the ponytail was acceptably attractive. The dressing was no problem, I stepped into an elegant low-cut black dress before I tried to walk in high heels. Luckily, the room had a carpet, so my wobbling backwards and forwards didn't disturb the occupants below on the third floor.

If walking in heels took some mastering, make-up was a nightmare. First, I applied too much eyes concealer and had to start again, then the foundation and a touch of blusher changed my appearance. I'd watched Alice apply these and use her little mascara brush, never thinking that one day I'd do the same. I looked in the dressing table mirror from every possible angle and liked what I saw. Afraid to undo my good work, I decided the final touch would be a long-lasting lipstick in discreet red.

I began to understand why Alice took so long to get ready whenever we went out. I resolved, there and then, I'd never chivvy her again. Finally, I attended to accessories, two gold-bar clip-on earrings, very pricey and pretty, a gold bracelet and an emerald solitaire ring: I'd splashed out on appearances. I just hoped that Sir Clive would create a curriculum worthy of my looks and IQ. Before going down in the lift, I sat down and practised crossing my legs or sitting with my knees together. As I did this, I rather lost myself in new ideas. One of these was that dear uncle Clive would have to organise some self-defence classes for me. I'd had no real agent training and now I wanted to learn to kill with my bare hands. If I was going to be MI5's answer to Nikita, I needed martial arts skills.

Pleased that I could walk confidently in my heels, my feminine figure meant that I had none of the problems male transvestites presumably encountered. A tall man with the build of a rugby player was standing by the lift. He was looking at the numbers changing above the door until I arrived. Then his attention shifted immediately to my cleavage but with a semblance of gentlemanly conduct looked straight up into my eyes.

"Good evening, miss, after you, please."

I slipped into the lift and gazing at my reflection as any normal woman would, I used the looking glass to study my companion. I found him quite attractive—oh dear, Jake Conley would have been repulsed!

"Ground floor, miss?"

"Oh yes, I'm on my way to the restaurant."

"Ah, what a happy coincidence, perhaps I could offer you an aperitif?"

I smiled and held his admiring gaze for just long enough before looking modestly at the floor. This being-a-woman business didn't appear so difficult.

"I think that would be lovely."

"Irish?"

"Yes, County Clare."

"That would account for it then."

"Sorry?"

"Your lovely auburn hair and blue eyes."

Confusion! I didn't know how to react; he was coming on too strongly, so, I opted for sarcasm.

"I see, a student of genetics, are you? Or is it a question of geography?"

"*Touché!* I deserved that. I didn't mean to be impertinent. Ah, we seem to have arrived! After you, again, miss."

"Jayne. Jayne Ryan."

"Pleased to meet you," he squeezed my fingers.

"Rob Sykes. I believe the bar is through there.

I chose a strawberry lemonade vodka largely because that's what Alice usually ordered. Apart from a new style of beverage, I'd have to become used to barmen devouring me with their eyes and the incessant male glances from every angle of the bar. I was secretly pleased when my cavalier asked what single malts the hotel offered and approved when he asked for a double Talisker, something I might have done myself in normal circumstances.

My next obstacle was to get used to my new voice. I didn't want to be too husky, but I should have had faith in my soft Irish brogue. Still, it takes some getting used to a female timbre. Certainly, I didn't want to have a strident laugh or to do anything that might incur the sort of harsh judgment males tend to reserve for unladylike women.

My first impression of Rob was correct. He was an amateur rugby player but luckily for me, after such a fortuitous encounter, he was excellent company. We dined together and I knew that he wanted more at the end of the evening, but I pleaded an important job interview the next day and the need for an early night—alone.

The relief of shaking free my hair, removing the pinching earrings and kicking off those infernal heels was exquisite. Lying in bed, thinking of my first day as a woman, I was very pleased with my ability to carry it off. But remembering that I *was* a real woman took some of the gloss off my performance. Before I fell asleep, I asked myself whether it would have been a betrayal of Alice if I'd had sex with Rob. Then I wondered whether my wife would like to play around with Jayne Ryan—I sincerely hoped not! As sleep overcame me, I was dreaming of my impact the next day on Sir Clive Cochrane.

I was still thinking about it after my morning shower and whilst pulling on a dark blue sheath dress that enhanced my figure and long legs. Applying make-up was a smoother operation than the previous day and soon I was ready to venture across the city. Getting in and out of the taxi was a skill I'd need to refine, given the tightness of my skirt. A quick visit to a photographer's for passport photos and I was on my way to the appointment with Sir Clive, the compliments of the photo expert still ringing in my ears.

My boss had a very different way of expressing admiration.

"Good God, Conley, I'd never have believed it possible! I say, isn't it a little over the top? On the other hand, Frankie Muir won't be able to keep his filthy paws off you."

I wasn't sure I appreciated the snigger. He continued,

Now look, Conley, or should I call you Jayne? I've prepared an outstanding curriculum for you. I spent half the night on it and it's a shoo-in for the high-level job for which I've recommended you. Now, my dear girl, except he pronounced it *gell*, I know you are blessed with an excellent intelligence quotient, so you'll be spending the next three days downstairs with Jeffrey Russell for an accelerated code-breaking course. I've put him in the picture, though not entirely, he thinks you are Jayne Ryan, a recruit to the service. I've told him that you'll be on an undercover operation and nobody must find gaps in your knowledge and competence. When you've finished your course, it's down to the basement with Park Mi-yeon for martial arts."

He gave me an encouraging smile, so I treated him to my prettiest pout and asked,

"Will there be an interview at GCHQ?"

"Well, there has to be, my dear, ahem, excuse the endearments, Conley—er—Jayne, but you *are* an enchanting creature. As I was saying, the usual recruitment, tough questions, background checks, Official Secrets Act and so on. But with the curriculum I've prepared you, you'd walk in even if you hadn't become such a strikingly attractive young woman."

"Thank you, sir. You say the sweetest things. I'll need a copy of the CV to examine in depth."

He slid a folder across the desk. "This contains the CV and a backstory for you about life in County Clare."

"What if they check up on my family there?"

"Well, of course, they'll find the Ryans. We'll just have to hope they don't dig too deeply about their non-existent daughter, Jayne. I'll have enough superficial false material put in place, such as baptism and other church certification, outstanding school record and whatnot. Now, I think you should hurry along to Russell and start mugging up."

"I'm afraid I can't, sir."

Hating contradiction, he let his gimlet eyes bore into mine.

"I beg your pardon?"

"Your door, sir. I struggle to open it as a man."

He chortled.

"Allow me, my dear," he heaved on his heavily-padded door and I observed with satisfaction the effort he too, had to put into opening it. I also noticed his gaze fixed on the rear of my tight dress.

Not even if you were the last man in the world...!

"Your British passport should be ready tomorrow and I'll keep you posted on your job application," he called after me. "Ah, Jayne!"

I turned to face him in the corridor.

"Sir?"

"Collect your new mobile from reception. It's safer to use a new number."

That was sensible of him. I was happy to take the lift down there but only wished the receptionist had been, as once before, the woman I'd fallen in love with. My mischievous Irish humour made me want to know how my wife would react to seeing the voluptuous new me.

"Please sign here, Ms Ryan."

I could see the receptionist's eyes searching for something to criticise, the mousy little creature! So, I gave her a winning smile and complimented her on her earrings. Even if I thought they were too long and heavy for her face-shape.

With her eyes on me as I returned to the lift with my mobile, I exaggerated the swing of my hips just for her, but the security guard's eyes widened dangerously, so I behaved myself.

As I rode up two floors, I worried that I'd be unable to assimilate the technical skills that were about to be thrust at me. But Jeff, as he wished me to call him, was a good-natured excellent communicator. He wasn't handsome in the classic sense, but rugged and tall with a small moustache that repelled me. This was all to the good because it helped my concentration. After three days, he was kind enough to tell me that I was the smartest student he'd had the pleasure to work with. I suspected some exaggeration, but not much because codebreaking fitted my personality perfectly. I'd grown up filling my spare time with cryptic crosswords, to pass the time of day, and enjoyed trying to solve Anglo-Saxon riddles. Pity I hadn't been involved at Bletchley Park in the Second World War. I'd have loved the thrill of deciphering Nazi codes.

Park Mi-yeon, as his name suggested, was Korean, but his English was perfect and his professionalism exemplary. He didn't blink when I told him what I needed: nothing more than to kill a man with my bare hand. A wicked sense of humour made him more endearing.

"Unfortunately, Miss, we're not allowed to use real men for you to practise on, I'm afraid you'll have to make do with dummies until I let you kill Malcolm."

"Malcolm? Who's he?"

"You can't meet him until you're proficient with the dummies. You might grow too fond of him." His eyes twinkled and I wondered what he had in mind.

First, he showed me anatomy charts and explained that when the carotid artery in the neck is struck with consummate force and accuracy, the blood flow to the brain is interrupted causing loss of consciousness or death.

"Extreme force and timing in precisely the right place, missie, that's the key to being lethal."

The white dummies were marked with a black dot and with the edge of my hand, I had to strike with all my might across the dot at an angle of forty-five degrees. My coach taught me to spin and deliver the blow or to lunge and hit the target. When I showed signs of sufferance, he had me do relaxation exercises and clenching and unclenching of my right hand. After hundreds of blows, he grunted in satisfaction.

"I believe you are ready to meet Malcolm."

I gaped at him in disbelief,

"Surely, you're not going to ask me to kill a real person?"

"But isn't that exactly why you came to me in the first place?" His tone became accusing, "Instead of letting me teach you self-defence... were you afraid I'd want to grapple with you on the floor?" The impish look had returned to his eye. "I'll just go and fetch Malcolm."

No, wait! I can't kill a man in cold blood.

Unvoiced, this sentiment remained unspoken because he had disappeared through a white door in the white wall that I hadn't noticed before. Waiting for him, I undid my elastic band and readjusted my hair, which with all the exertion had become disordered. One needed to look one's best when killing a man!

Mi-yeon returned with his arm supporting the fellow, whom he seemed to be dragging like a dead weight. Was that it? Had he raided the morgue for Malcolm?

"Meet Malcolm," the Korean chuckled, "He's an android fitted with sensors, capable of registering the efficacy of your blow."

Phew!

"What I want you to do, Miss Ryan, is to stand there so you can't see Malcolm, yes, just so. On the count of five, spin and strike to kill. One-two-three-four *five*! There was no time to think and no bloody black dot! I struck where I would have done on the dummy's throat. To achieve sufficient force, I kept Frankie Muir in mind.

"Splendid blow, missie! Let's see the printout. He let go of the android that he'd been keeping upright and pressed a button on a control panel in its back. A whirring followed by the familiar jerky sound of a printer ended with the trainer tearing off a strip of paper.

"Amazing! Congratulations! According to this, you not only severely damaged the artery but you also fractured two bones in the neck beyond it. I've had many trainees, Miss Ryan, but few have emerged, like you, as a professional assassin."

"T-thank you," I said, feeling giddy and happy to know that I could destroy Muir with one hand when the opportunity arose.

TWENTY-ONE
CHELTENHAM SPA, GCHQ, DECEMBER 2022

My first impression was the size of the structure as I approached. At a guess, it was as big as our national football stadium and about the same shape. What a glance didn't reveal was that this was a hub, connecting its workers with satellites and ground stations covering every square inch of our planet—a giant ear. This place was designed to eavesdrop on military, commercial and even diplomatic communications and the irony was, inside reigned a cynic sworn to protect the United Kingdom and its citizens, but at the same time, preparing to sacrifice eighty per cent of them. And here was I, about to attempt to penetrate this top-security citadel. True, I'd do it in the name of its avowed ideals but, paradoxically, by subterfuge.

Seldom have I felt so vulnerable as I opened my bag at the entrance under the scrutiny of the guard to produce my official pass. He read it, cross-checked it and ticked his list.

I'm not sure what he scrutinised more, the document or the woman in front of him. Today, I'd chosen to power dress in a sober grey pinstripe trouser suit, on one lapel a silver art deco dragonfly made a statement. He gazed appraisingly and said,

"If you'll just fill in this form, Ms Ryan, stating the nature of your business in the last section."

Two minutes, and I'd completed the simple questionnaire and handed it over.

He glanced at it, tore off the top part along the perforations and placed it in a tray.

"Job interview, miss? Well, good luck! I hope you get it; it'll help brighten up the place."

He was looking at me like a famished wolf might eye a rabbit. In his hand, the plastic clip-on badge blaring VISITOR PASS in orange letters hung between us like an unexploded grenade. Would he risk my wrath by trying to clip it on or, simply, as decorum required, hand it over? Wisely, on seeing the ice in my eyes, he opted for the latter and I attached it to my other lapel. Picking up an internal phone, he announced my arrival.

"Someone will be down in a couple of minutes, miss. Please wait over there."

A young woman wearing a cream blouse and black skirt and tights appeared and exchanged a nod and smile with the guard.

"Ms Ryan?" she extended a hand and I squeezed her fingers, "Come this way."

She swiped a plastic card through a box on the wall and a panel slid silently open. We stepped through into a room with lockers and several chairs, where two women and a man were studying me from head to toe and a low table bearing tidy piles of scientific magazines.

My guide indicated a locker, "All electronic equipment, jewellery and handbag in there, please Ms Ryan, regulations, you know."

"Your watch, as well, I'm afraid." She sounded apologetic.

I smiled and said, "Of course. But I'm hardly presentable now."

"God help the rest of us then," she said in a low voice.

"How very sweet of you!"

Her smile was genuine, reaching her eyes.

"Do take a seat. I think they'll call you in alphabetical order."

The others were candidates for my job. What a shame for them...

I'd studied my CV and read Sir Clive's glowing reference. Most of all, I could count on the support of Sir Samuel Blackwell, a.k.a. Lugus. They weren't going to give in without a fight: quite rightly. The man was the first to speak.

"I don't think we should sit here in silence till we go crazy!"

I reacted first, smiling at him, "So, what do you propose, Mr...?"

"Banks, David, by name."

So, he'll be going in first!

"I'm Jayne Ryan, pleased to meet you."

"Irish?" He raised an eyebrow, "I thought only British nationals—oh, I see you're from *Northern Ireland.*"

I let him think what he liked; it didn't make any difference. He was a trier, I had to concede when he turned to the blonde next to him,

"You're not Welsh or something, are you?"

"If I were, I don't think I'd take kindly to the question," she said archly.

I took to her on the instant.

"My name's Beryl Beecham, so I guess you get in before me, Mr Banks."

"By a whisker!" he grinned. "It might not be such an advantage to be first, though...unless..." he turned to the elegant dark-haired woman sitting next to me, "is your surname Abbott or Arbuthnot?" he chuckled at his witticism.

"I wish," she said, "I'm third, unfortunately." She turned to smile at me, "For us, the torture is prolonged! Oh, I'm Catherine Hogg, until I get married and get rid of it." She giggled.

Don't fall in love with Mr Pigby!

I liked the women but David Banks grated on me. Luckily, he was first alphabetically, so we'd all be left in peace. In a place like this, they'd separate us after the interview, surely. I'd probably have been nervous if I'd been a genuine candidate but as it was, I was cool and relaxed. Which is most likely why he tried to get under my skin.

"So, Miss Ryan, coming to work for the perpetrators of Bloody Sunday, are you?"

I stared at him until he could hold my gaze no longer.

"There are many English people dismayed at what happened in the Bogside in 1972...and then there are *eejits like youse*, who're prepared to joke about twenty-six deaths."

He reddened and glared.

"I say, no need to be offensive!"

The blonde stared at him and showing remarkable solidarity, said,

"Quite honestly, David, you're the one who's been objectionable from the start. We'll put it down to pre-interview nerves."

Beryl was so sympathetic, I felt bad about cheating her out of a job.

Twenty minutes between candidates, so after an hour, the secretary in the cream blouse called me in. Three men were sitting behind a desk, one with a fountain pen poised over a pad. I recognised Sir Samuel Blackwell, whose stony countenance sowed no flicker of recognition, although I was sure Sir Clive would have put him in the picture; the hatchet-faced Francis Muir was the one in the middle. The absence of white face paint did little to improve his looks. They all held high-ranking positions in GCHQ and Muir introduced them, finishing with his position,

"...Chief Executive Officer, responsible for the running of the National Cyber Security Centre. Which means that if you are offered the post, Ms Ryan, I will be your direct superior. Now..."

He went on to explain the importance of intercepting material and stopping others stealing data: the invaluable contribution of safeguarding current systems, communications and electronic data. He ended his hypocritical spiel by saying,

"Your curriculum suggests you are fitted to working in our department. How do you feel about, let's say, the more politically sensitive nature of our work?"

He means he doesn't want any Red Flag flying in my head.

I'd done my homework, so I looked him in the eyes before meeting the gaze of the other two,

"I think that all the requisite controls are in place, gentlemen, the government-appointed Intelligence and Security Committee regularly scrutinises your work to ensure that activities are always authorised, necessary and proportionate. I know what I'm signing up for and I'm as fierce a patriot as anyone in this room, respectfully speaking."

I caught my breath, wondering if I'd overdone it. Apparently not, because they went on to ask the usual interview questions, why I thought I was suitable, what I considered my strengths and so on.

"Well, gentlemen," said Muir, "unless Ms Ryan has anything further she'd like to ask us, I think we can close there."

"No, Sir Francis, thank you, I think everything's clear in my mind."

"We will now need to discuss the candidates, my dear"—it was his first endearment but he'd been eying my thighs longingly throughout— "we'll let you know our decision soon."

His smile was encouraging but...with that CV, I had few doubts, how could I fail?

I was conducted back to the same waiting room and I had no idea what had happened to the other three candidates. To pass the time I picked up a copy of New Scientist and began to read an article entitled **The Mystery of the Missing Quarks**.

Sir Francis, in person, entered the room to interrupt my reading. I guess the missing quarks will remain a mystery to me forever. His smile veered on the edge of leering and his tone was friendly.

"Congratulations, my dear, you have the job. We were very impressed and you'll be expected to begin a brief induction course on Monday. First, there are one or two formalities to complete, but perhaps I might have the honour of inviting you to lunch. We have an excellent restaurant on the premises. I'm sure you would like a look around, so it will be my privilege to be your Cicero—ahem, if you take my meaning?"

I did, but it was just his pompous way of saying, 'I'll show you round the joint'. I can't bear pomposity, so, I hit back by quoting the great orator:

"*Live as brave men; and if fortune is adverse, front its blows with brave hearts.*"

"My word! I can see we've selected a treasure for ourselves! Come this way please." He placed a hand on the small of my back and steered me towards the wall. His hand went limp and he let it slide down over my buttock. I could have spun and struck the deadly blow there and then, but it wouldn't have served our purposes. *This was not the place to conclude the business.*

Despite irritation at this molestation, I not only controlled my reflexes but also my tongue. Letting him think he could take liberties had to be part of my plan. At the wall, he used a magnetic card to open a sliding door and we strolled into a shiny corridor.

"As you can see, Jayne"—he hadn't bothered to ask permission to use my given name— "the architecture is in a circular layout…"

It looked like a shopping centre to me, but one without the shops. He continued, "…off this outer corridor, the doors lead to work areas. You'll have a personal pass. Nobody may enter without authorisation. Let's take this entrance. He swiped his card."

It led to a large room where hundreds of people were sitting at computers and for a place containing so many people, there was little noise. Everyone concentrated on his task. Suddenly, as they walked past the computer stations, I felt overdressed. Most of the employees were dressed casually, some even in jeans: admittedly, with designer labels.

I noticed that whenever we came close to a screen, it would go blank or a screensaver would take over. When I drew Sir Francis's attention to this, he stopped strolling and whispered,

"In a place like ours, we have to take every precaution. They will have asked you to leave your mobile. Had you somehow managed to enter with it, it would not function; instead, it would be automatically blocked."

"Sensible precautions, you never know who you can trust."

He glanced at me with a curious expression.

"My dear Jayne, I repeat, we have found ourselves a treasure! By the way, you never did accept my invitation."

"Forgive me. I must have been distracted. Lunch? Yes, that would be delightful."

"Splendid!"

He pointed and my gaze followed his outstretched finger. There was a note of pride.

"The wall you see there, in the centre of the room is steel and concrete-lined. We call it 'The Cage'. It's a kind of inner sanctum and is completely autonomous and sealed off from the rest of the building. Even in the event of a terrorist attack..." I gasped, "... oh, forgive me, my dear, I didn't mean to frighten you...it won't happen...but hypothetically speaking, no hostile person could penetrate that room. In there, we have a coding machine that encrypts all MI6 and MI5 files."

He spoke with such fervour and pride that I began to doubt my knowledge of his true character, which I would have to try to bring out soon, as time was pressing. We were just a fortnight away from the solstice.

Next on the itinerary was the gym.

"Oh, yes, I work out every morning before I start the day. *Mens sana in corpore sano*, and all that." Again, he took the opportunity to study my figure. "It would seem you adhere to the same principle, Jayne."

"Well, I go for a run every morning."

"Good for you, but now you're our employee, why don't you join me at eight o'clock? I assure you, the treadmills are state of the art."

To ogle me in shorts and a T-shirt, you dirty old dog.

"That would be delightful."

For the moment, I had to keep in his good books. My intensive background study paid off over lunch because he interrogated me about my upbringing. Pleased to find that I was single, he chanced his arm by inviting me to dinner one evening.

"Perhaps later in the week, Sir Francis, if you don't mind. I have to settle into my new job and it may be tiring for the first few days."

I signed my contract and The Official Secrets Act and left the building in a jubilant mood.

My only worry was that the solstice was drawing ever nearer and I needed to work my way so far into Muir's confidence that he would involve me in his scheme. Whatever the cost? Back in my hotel, I worked on that. The dinner out I'd delayed, but after that evening out, what then? I might need an exit strategy.

Two days of induction and he summoned me to his office. He asked me to sit down and I took a chair opposite his desk. I crossed my legs, revealing rather a lot of thigh and watched for his appreciative gaze. That out of the way, he began,

"You look ravishing this morning, my dear."

"It must be the work-out and the shower, Sir Francis."

"I have a report here from your cypher instructor."

My heart rate quickened and I held my breath as I could afford no failure.

"I keep saying we've found a treasure! It would appear that your intelligence matches your stunning looks."

Air surged out of my nostrils and I fancy that I blushed even if I hated him.

"You say the most flattering things," I looked at him from under my lowered brow.

Moving to a side cabinet, he opened it and took out two glasses. They were champagne flutes.

"Damn the calories!"

Bending down, he took out a bottle from a fridge. I glimpsed a green label with a stylised golden S.

"You will join me." It wasn't a question.

"Are we celebrating, sir?"

"Perspicacious as ever, my dear Jayne. I've decided to make you my PA."

I gasped.

"Does that please you? I see it does! And what better way to seal a pact than a bottle of Salon Blanc de Blancs Le Mesnil-sur-Oger, 1997?"

A flawless French accent was to be expected from one with his educational background but that was the only unexpected aspect of this tableau. Things had fallen so dramatically into place that I couldn't help looking delighted. Of course, he flattered himself thinking that any young woman would be pleased to be his personal assistant. To be fair, he'd kept himself in good shape for his age, but his hatchet face and the hardness of his eyes too often gave him a grim or hostile expression. The thought of his inevitable assault on my virtue filled me with loathing but for the moment, things were going well.

TWENTY-TWO
CHELTENHAM SPA, GCHQ DECEMBER 2022 AD

On my first day of work and proudly displaying my employee pass to the same guard at the entrance, in return, I received a leer and a cheery,

"I see you got the job, miss. Congratulations! I'll look forward to seeing *you* every day."

I gave him my icy stare and watched him wilt.

"I know you will," I said and breezed past, thinking how much patience it took to be a pretty woman or in my case, a beautiful one. Regulations required me to leave my jewellery and electronic equipment, in this case, my mobile. But knowing this, I had come without accessories. I put the numbered key in my pocket and tried to remember my way to Sir Francis's office but took the wrong door by triumphantly swiping my magnetic card. In moments, I realised I was lost but spotted salvation immediately in the shape of Aria Gough. He was a good test of my appearance.

"Excuse me," he looked up irritated from his screen that had gone blank, but the annoyance changed instantly to male interest. I hadn't been a woman long but I recognised that *undressing you with his eyes look*. And shame on him, married to the lovely Ishbe. Appraisal over, he asked,

"Can I help you, miss?"

He had no idea he was speaking to Jake Conley, of course.

I blushed and admitted, "How stupid of me. It's my first day of work and I'm lost in this labyrinth."

"Where is it you should be?"

"I'm Sir Francis Muir's PA and should be at his office."

Aria's face clouded at the mention of his name, but was too wise to make an unguarded statement,

"I'll be pleased to show you the way, miss."

He stood and offered a hand. "Aria Gough. I'm just a menial here."

I took the proffered hand and squeezed the fingers, "I'm sure you're frightfully good at your work, Mr Gough. It's very kind of you. Jayne Ryan."

Outside Sir Francis's door, he hesitated.

"Very nice to meet you, Ms Ryan. If you ever need a friendly ear or advice—"

He seemed to want to say more but I didn't want him to compromise himself,

"I see by your ring that you're married, Mr Gough."

His face fell and I could have laughed.

"Just remember the offer, Ms Ryan."

I thanked him and he departed whilst I knocked on the door and was admitted.

"I'm sorry. I hope I'm not late. I got lost and had to be escorted to your door."

He glanced at his watch.

"You are ten minutes *early*, Jayne. I appreciate punctuality but," his eyes rested on my décolletage, "I must say, I was disappointed not to see you in the gym this morning."

"I need to get my routine organised, sir. What, with travel in and finding my bearings. I'll try to be there tomorrow at eight o'clock."

"Splendid! Now, as I prefer to know everything about my employees, I'm going to sit you down in an empty room and give you these to complete. He handed me a folder, which I supposed must contain some work for GCHQ. How wrong can you be?

When he'd settled me with a pen and paper in a nearby office, he said, you have half an hour to finish the first one. When it's done, bring it to me."

He closed the door and I opened the yellow folder to find an intelligence test. Surely, my CV was sufficient. I racked my brain for anything that I might have led him to believe my IQ was other than high but failed to come up with an answer. I sighed and looked at the printed material. The Stanford-Binet Intelligence Test—I'd never heard of it, but hurried through the first page filled with typical questions to test reasoning, knowledge, visual-spatial processing, and, I supposed working memory. I found most of them easy. I knew I would. I recalled a fifth-form teacher insisting I should join Mensa, although my IQ had never been formally tested. At the time, I turned it down, I was already a quiet introspective pupil and didn't want to be even more different from my classmates.

I was a little distracted as to why my new boss wished to know my IQ, which meant that I had to re-read a couple of questions. The ones that gave me pause for thought were finding the number that didn't belong in the series. Each time, I was cross with myself because when I caught on, it was obvious. I'd left my watch in the locker, but the room had a wall clock and I realised I'd finished the test, despite the occasional distraction, within twenty minutes.

My heels clicked along the corridor and I knocked.

"Come!"

I've always hated the single word command, but smiled sweetly and laid the yellow folder on his desk.

He glanced at his watch again,

"All done, my dear. Here's another one. Can't just rely on one, however good it is."

He handed over another folder—red this time.

Something in my expression must have alerted him,

"Humour me, my dear, there's method in my madness!"

"Whatever you say, sir."

It didn't matter, as I'd always enjoyed quizzes, tests and riddles. Besides, I was being paid very well to enjoy myself, but I was irritated not knowing what method lay behind his seemingly irrational demands. I'd read something about Weschler once and remembered that he was an advocate for the concept of non-intellective factors. He argued that, what he revealed to be the Binet, test I'd just completed did not do a good job of incorporating these factors into the scale; non-intellective factors are variables that contribute to the overall score in intelligence but are not made up of intelligence-related items. These include things such as lack of confidence, fear of failure, attitudes, and so on.

I rattled through this test, enjoying it more than the previous one since I found it more challenging. Sir Francis, surprised to see me so soon, gave me a curious stare. I saw that he was checking the yellow folder.

"Off you go, my dear, I'll want you back in half an hour. Go get yourself a coffee and don't get lost on the way!"

He chuckled and I walked out stiff-shouldered and silent. I remembered the way back to Aria's work area and retraced the route. Exactly why, I'm not sure. Maybe I felt in need of a friendly face. I found it, but not his: his wife's. Ishbel! I couldn't let her know I knew her but coffee with her would be pleasant.

"Excuse me, I'm new here. Is there a coffee bar or dispenser anywhere?"

As I'd hoped, she stood and said,

"I'm gasping for one myself. Come on, we can go together."

I'd always liked Ishbel and appreciated her spontaneous friendliness with an unknown glamorous woman. "Which department are you in?"

"I'm Sir Francis Muir's PA, as from today."

I saw the flash of repugnance, well disguised, but there, nonetheless.

Should I risk a comment? But she beat me to it.

"I'd be interested to know what you think of him after a few weeks. He's frightfully intelligent, of course, but not to everyone's liking."

"I guess I can put you in that group, miss...?"

"Oh, I'm married, Mrs Gough, but call me Ishbel."

"Pretty name. Scottish?"

"Yes, by ancestry. I can hear you're Irish."

"I hope my accent isn't too strong. I'm Jayne. It's on the badge, Jayne Ryan."

"So I see. And no, it's a lovely lilt. I quite envy you. I might have guessed from your hair colouring even before you spoke. We Celts should stick together, Jayne."

"I'd like that, Ishbel. I have no friends here."

She smiled gaily,

"Well, it's early days," she steered me into the restaurant and towards a bar in the corner, "someone with your looks will soon have more than he can cope with."

"That's sweet of you, Ishbel."

We joined the short queue and she whispered, "On that score, be warned, Muir's a terrible womaniser."

"Oh, is he married?"

She frowned, "Not as far as I know. Let me get these. Sugar? Silly question. Two expressos. I noticed she didn't use money but handed her magnetic card to the barista."

So that's how it works.

"Thanks, Ishbel."

We sat down, more for a chat than for the coffee.

"What does your husband do?"

"Aria? He works here, too. Something to do with cyphering."

"In the Cage?"

"Good heaven, no. Not far from where you met me."

"Oh, that's handy. Tell me more about Sir Francis. You have me worried."

She smiled and took my hand, "I didn't mean to interfere. It's just that..."

"Yes?"

"Well, there was some fuss with lawyers and, you know, that sort of thing is frowned on here. For a lesser being than the high and mighty Sir Francis," her voice was almost inaudible, "it would lead to immediate dismissal. There was some trouble with one of our female programmers. She cited him for molestation. She simply disappeared from GCHQ and we've lost all track of her. I guess it was all hushed up and settled out of court."

"I'll have to keep him at arm's length. Thanks for the warning."

"You're welcome. Where are you living, Jayne?"

"For the moment I'm still in a hotel, the Best Western. But I'm looking for a bedsit."

We chatted for a while, she giving me advice and offered to have me round to her place for tea and cake. I accepted gracefully for the following week.

Making no mistake with my route back to Sir Francis's office, I knocked precisely after half an hour.

"Come! My dear Jayne, do sit. I'm never wrong about these things, you know! I said we'd found ourselves a treasure. Do you know, you scored one hundred and thirty-six on the Weschler Adult Intelligence Scale, which puts you firmly in the top 0.1 per cent of the population and registers as *very superior*.

"One hundred and thirty-six?" I looked and sounded disappointed.

He chortled, "Oh no, dear Jayne, that is *not* your IQ. That came out at one hundred and sixty-eight. My dear girl, you do realise that makes you practically a *genius!*"

"Oh, that's nice!"

I tried to do my best to look astonished and humble.

"Now, Jayne, there are some things we must talk about, which do not concern work. Don't leap to the wrong conclusions, I'm not making advances, although when we've got to know each other better..." he paused and gave me an oily smile that caused an internal shudder, "...I'll now have to show you the outstanding work we—*I*—have to catch up on... but this other matter. I need to have you to myself for an evening. I already proposed dinner some time and you gave me a very professional reason," he smiled ingratiatingly, "for putting it back. But time isn't on my side. I would like it very much, Jayne, if we could dine together tomorrow."

My breathing became more rapid. He'd said time wasn't on his side. Was he referring to the approaching solstice? I believed so.

"That would be delightful, sir."

"Ah, my dear girl, you've made me very happy. Now, shall we say I'll pick you up at 8.00 pm? Where would be convenient?"

"I'm staying at the Best Western Hotel, handy for work...it's a temporary arrangement."

"Ah, of course. I'll be there at eight then. Let's get to work."

I was soon immersed in his world of communications, organising future meetings, conferences and gala dinners. When I studied the monthly planner, I realised with a start that the days around the full moon were the only ones completely free of engagements. I didn't comment on this.

At lunchtime, I found Ishbel and Aria and asked to join them. His wife was surprised that we'd already met and we laughed, me having found only *them* out of the six thousand employees working in the Doughnut.

Ishbel became serious and Aria edgy when I told them Sir Francis had invited me out for dinner the next evening.

"He'll take you to some swish restaurant and ply you with charm and oodles of alcohol," she warned.

"Don't worry, I'm *Oirish* and can drink himself under the table!" I joked.

Aria looked as if he wanted to change the subject.

"So, how was your first morning, Ms Ryan?"

"Weird. He tested my IQ. Is it standard practice? I didn't know whether to be insulted."

They both looked perplexed.

"It's a new one on me," he said, "So, how was it?"

"Aria! Really!" Ishbel hissed.

I smiled, "He seemed impressed."

I wasn't about to make myself unpopular—dealing with an IQ of 168 would put most people on the defensive.

The rest of my working day passed pleasantly and I spent much of it organising my workspace, which was connected to the Director's office by an internal door. I was looking forward to my evening in the hotel and considering how to formulate my urgent request to Sir Clive when a knock came at the door. It wasn't Sir Francis; he would just breeze in as if by right. Instead, I was pleased to see Sir Samuel Blackwell.

He slid into the office quickly and looking furtively around whispered,

"Are you really Jake Conley?"

It was understandable if his mind really couldn't take in this transformation.

"Yes, I can tell you anything you like about our meeting in St Mary de Lode church in Gloucester."

His mouth dropped open, "Good Lord! So, it's true—quite amazing, so how's it going, Jake – er – Jayne."

"Be careful not to slip up, sir, it's going very well, so far. I think I'll get him where I want him."

"Good man! Er-woman!"

This wasn't good enough and I'd have expected better from someone so high-powered. It had to be shock at my transformation. My anxiety increased when the inner door opened and Sir Francis came in. He glared at Sir Samuel.

"What're you doing here, Sammy? Not chatting up my PA, I hope."

"Good heavens, no! Just popped by to see how Ms Ryan's first day had gone. I'll be off now"—he pronounced it *orf*.

Sir Francis waited for the door to be closed.

"Be wary of him, Jayne. He snoops around a lot, you know... mum's the word!

That Muir was suspicious of Sir Samuel surprised me but knowing their opposing philosophies made it easier to understand. I would have to warn Blackwell to watch his step, via Sir Clive—another thing to add to the evening phone call.

After a relaxing shower, I made up and chose a change of clothes with a black lace puff sleeve top and matching black linen blend tapered trousers. Then, I sat to brush my hair: my long, straight auburn crowning glory, I wore it completely loose save for two small tortoiseshell clips above my temples to hold it away from my face and forehead, and then added my gold bar earrings. Finally, I slipped my feet into a pair of black leather buckle slingbacks. I stood in front of the mirror and admired the effect. I didn't intend to be a woman much longer but at least I'd enjoy my beauty whilst I could.

On the way to the restaurant, I revelled in the admiring glances, not just from men either. It seemed a shame to dine alone but although I tried the bar, looking for Rob, there was no sign of him. At the reception desk, they informed me that Mr Sykes had checked out that morning, so I'd have to make the best of my own company.

I decided the way to do that was to order a chilled white wine, which would wash down the *pan-fried sea bass with prawn risotto and chive and herb oil*. As I ate this delicious dish, I reflected that maybe it was better that Rob had gone. We would surely have finished in bed and sex as a woman was something of which I had no experience. The more I thought about it, the less the idea appealed to me. Anyway, I needed total privacy to call Sir Clive Cochrane.

The young, tall waiter, I decided from his looks, an Italian, solicitous in topping up my glass took my plate, recited the desserts available and looked pleased when I ordered the *chef's homemade lemon tart served with fruit compote*.

"A very good choose, *signora*," he said in approximate English.

I discovered that his name was Danilo and he was only twenty-two, from a village in Umbria, near Spoleto. This showed how much I felt in need of conversation after my day in GCHQ. I tipped him £10 and forgave him his hungry ogling—I was too old and sophisticated for him anyway.

Placing the Do Not Disturb sign on the handle, I locked the door carefully and tapped in Sir Clive's number on the mobile he'd provided.

"Ah, *Jayne* ho-ho, how nice to hear from you, dear *gell*, how's it going?"

"Better than hoped, sir. I got the job and instant promotion to Muir's PA—"

"By Jove! Did you, indeed?"

I wasn't sure how much I wanted to say on the phone and would have to resort to coded speech.

"You might have to send the cleaners tomorrow evening. I'll text the address and let them in myself."

There was a long silence.

"I think a flight abroad for one of our boys armed with a passport in Frankie's name might be a good idea under the circumstances. Better go now and set the wheels in motion. Oh, and Jayne, good work!"

Well, it would be if I could pull it off. The *cleaners* would remove and dispose of the body. I texted Sir Francis's address and without further thoughts, undressed and opted for an early night.

Amazingly, on the eve of becoming an executioner, I slept as soundly as a hibernating brown bear.

TWENTY-THREE
WORCESTERSHIRE, DECEMBER 2022 AD

Reception knew that I was expecting a car at 8.00 pm so they phoned my room,

"Your car has arrived, Ms Ryan."

I put the last touch to my lipstick and grabbed my silver evening bag. Studying the effect in the mirror, I smiled approval at my low-cut black sheath gown and the usual gold-bar earrings. How would I ever do without them when I returned to being Jake?

In the foyer, I had the surprise of a uniformed chauffeur, who escorted me to the waiting Mercedes. It set the tone for the evening and freed Sir Francis's hands so that one was soon resting on my knee and I had to remove it when it began to venture higher.

The restaurant must have been the most exclusive in the county. Already, before we were escorted to our tables, champagne arrived in an ice bucket in a private lounge with sumptuous furnishings. The attentive waiters all addressed Sir Francis by his name, which led me to ask mischievously,

"They seem to know you well, Sir Francis. Do you bring all of your conquests here?"

He looked abashed,

"Good heavens, no. I come here for business dinners, usually in an all-male company. Do you take me for a Lothario?"

The best way to redirect the conversation was to dazzle him,

"Have you read *The Fair Penitent*, Sir Francis?"

"I'm not fond of eighteenth-century literature, Jayne, but am suitably impressed by your cultural preparation."

Condescending swine!

The meal lived up to the superb setting of damasked wallpaper, velvet padded chairs, brilliant silverware and porcelain. My cavalier displayed a connoisseur's knowledge of wine to ensure perfect pairing throughout the courses. When he was sure that I was sufficiently relaxed, he made his first attempt to read my mind. I couldn't simply block him or it would alert him to my powers, so I distracted him by thinking flattering thoughts about him and laid it on thick.

Luckily, it worked and he stopped his mental probing. He was a powerful shaman and I would have to be careful, especially with what I had in mind. Confident in my unwound and receptive state, he launched into the true purpose of the evening.

"You might be wondering, Jayne, how I had the effrontery to subject you to an intelligence test. I must apologise; I admit it is not standard practice, but I have great plans for you—for us". I sat up and feigned close attention. "What is your opinion of democracy, my dear?"

I frowned and thought it better to be straightforward,

"It's a difficult question in the middle of an exquisite meal, but I'll try to answer. Democracy has its weaknesses, but it is still superior to totalitarianism: fascism or communism—"

I hadn't finished, but he seized on the first part of my reply,

"Ah, exactly, it has its weaknesses. What would you say are the main ones?"

I knew where he was heading with this and would have to string him along.

"Even the first democracy, the Athenian one, was open to only thirty per cent of the population. It excluded women and those without property. Nowadays everyone can vote and as we live in a period of mass culture, unfortunately even the most ignorant is enfranchised."

"Precisely, which means a young woman with your intelligence has her vote cancelled by some pot-bellied, skin-headed layabout with the brain of a sparrow. I and a group of close friends are working on this problem, Jayne. If you think that only twenty per cent of the population has the acumen to understand the implications of voting and that a very small part of these, who I'll call *Brain Lords*, are suitable to rule, then we have a revolutionary interpretation of democracy."

"But surely, the other eighty per cent will not stand by to see their democratic rights abrogated?"

"Imagine a scenario where they have no choice because survival will be their only preoccupation."

I had him where I wanted him, condemning himself with every word, but still, I played along.

"Is this possible?" I looked incredibly impressed.

He smiled reassuringly,

"Yes, my dear. It is likely, nay, certain. A world-shattering event is only a matter of days away."

There was a fanatical light in his eyes. "And you have been selected to be part of this renaissance. But look, I mustn't spoil our cosy evening. I think we can talk about this more comfortably in my home later on."

"Oh, won't you be taking me back to my hotel?" I asked innocently.

"If that is what you want, then, of course. I had hoped to show you my house. It's in Dutch colonial-style. I'm sure you'll like it. Also, I have some very advantageous propositions for you."

Providing I shed my knickers!

I put on a brave, intrigued face.

"Well then, *that* is what we will do, Sir Francis."

He beamed and once more eyed my décolletage. There could be no doubt what I was walking into.

The chauffeur was a complication I hadn't reckoned on, but I felt sure I could handle the situation. Especially after the Mercedes glided through the ornate gates when I glimpsed the large house and naively asked,

"Goodness, there must be a lot of people in there."

"No, my dear," he was holding my hand, "the staff do not live in. They will all be safely abed in the village. We shall be quite alone."

"Except for your driver."

"He will park the car in the garage and return with his own to his wife."

"Ah."

Does that bother you, Jayne?"

"Oh no, you have been the perfect gentleman, Sir Francis; I'm sure I can find a way of repaying you for such a splendid evening."

"I'm sure you can!"

It was impossible to miss the excitement in his tone.

He managed to contain himself long enough to offer his exceptional whisky. I pretended shock.

"I've never tasted whisky in my life," I lied, "I think it would go straight to my head."

"Surely not. This is no cheap plonk. It will warm you and help you to relax."

When we finished the excellent tipple, he suggested,

"Let me show you around my home."

He ignored the kitchen and headed for the stairs.

"Please ignore this breach of etiquette, my dear. I'll lead the way. Strictly speaking, manners insist that a gentleman should follow the lady on a staircase, should she stumble. But as the house is unknown to you..."

It wasn't mysterious to me at all, I'd been there as Jake, but true, I hadn't ventured upstairs. He went straight to the bedroom to display a four-poster bed with pride. The sheets were black silk and above them a luxurious pearl Icelandic quilted eiderdown.

"You'll be quite snug in there, Jayne. Take your clothes off."

Just like that—the only unsophisticated words he'd uttered all evening. I gulped and unzipped my gown, letting it slide down to my ankles. Now it was his turn to swallow hard as I had no need for a bra and wasn't wearing one.

"Oh, my dear, but you are Aphrodite in person! Exquisite...words fail me."

Judging by the bulge in his trousers, not everything failed him.

I rolled down my stockings, kicked off my shoes and removed my slip whilst he struggled frantically to undress.

I slipped into bed and watched the rest of the performance. If my spirit had been female, I'd have found his body less repulsive than his mind. He was in great shape for his age. As it was, I was like a coiled spring. The situation was repellent.

He joined me in bed and pressing my velvety flesh next to his body, I could feel the urgency of his desire. I pushed him away, and with an icy look said,

"So, you and your friends are planning to write off four-fifths of the population. Do you think you'll be allowed to do that and get away with it?"

Alerted by my glacial eyes and tone, he did precisely what I wanted from him: he sat up.

"Who *are* you?" His last words on earth.

Fast as a cobra, I struck unerring as I'd trained for this exact moment. The blow was powered by all the hatred for this fiend that I'd stored up.

There was no point in checking as I knew he was dead—and the world was a better place for it. Still, for a scruple, after I'd dressed, I put my fingertips to his neck and verified the absence of a pulse. I took my mobile from my pochette and rang Sir Clive.

"Could you send the cleaners? There are no complications. I'll wait here until they arrive. I was thinking, could word leak out that

Sir Francis has abandoned everything to live with his personal assistant in some tropical retreat? I don't intend to remain Jayne Ryan for much longer. It's not an easy life, sir, being a beauty."

What was he gurgling at the other end of the line? He should be very pleased that I'd carried out the operation without a hitch. At last, he returned to the efficient mode I knew so well.

"The cleaners will be with you within twenty minutes. I had them positioned on standby."

That was what I wanted to hear and sure enough, after a quarter of an hour, a vehicle was flashing its headlights through the wrought iron gates. It had taken me ten minutes to work out the control panel in the hall, but having done so, I operated the gates and let the driver bring the plain black van to the front door. A team of three men approached and I showed them to the bedroom. Their leader looked at me perplexed.

"No blood ma'am?"

I smiled, "No just a chop to the carotid artery."

He gaped, "You mean—"

The same sweet smile, "Don't say it, please. Yes, a *woman* killed a man with her bare hands."

He looked awestruck and gulped.

"Well that's what I trained to do," I said innocently.

The three men exchanged looks but then they snapped into professional mode. Out came the black body bag and they put the hatchet-faced cadaver inside and zipped it up. One of them folded and hung up the various items of clothing. The tie went in the appropriate drawer, the shoes in the wardrobe.

"You made our job easy ma'am. Now, try to remember everything you touched in this house."

I recited everything I'd handled from entering, so they washed and dried and replaced the whisky glasses, wiped the control panel and satisfied, the leader said,

"I think we can go, lads, ma'am. But wait! Someone will have to close the gates after us or it'll look suspicious tomorrow if they're wide open."

"I'll do it," I said.

"Here, wear this, we don't want any prints."

Pulling on a latex glove, I watched them drive out and pull up, then closed the gate. The pedestrian exit opened from the inside only, so I quickly joined them and asked to be taken to my hotel.

"What will you do with the body?" I asked the team leader.

"We'll take him to the Department's morgue. After that, I've no idea what happens to the stiffs and to be honest, I don't care. I wouldn't worry your pretty head."

He almost bit off the last words and looked anxiously at me.

"It's cool, I like a compliment as much as the next girl—if it's from the right source and, I'm pleased to have you fellows tidy up for me."

He looked at me and asked in almost a whisper, "Do you mind me asking, ma'am, do you do this kind of operation often?"

"When required," I said, my tone blasé.

"So how many...?"

"Oh, I've lost count," I lied, putting this mischievousness down to the evening's drinking and a touch of Munchausen syndrome.

"I can understand how your targets must let their guard down," he whispered, "I mean, most men would look at those delicate arms and never believe..."

"Yes, it's an advantage, but look, I think we've arrived. Better if you drop me here and I'll walk in. They'd be expecting something more luxurious than a black van."

I rewarded him with a kiss on the cheek and hoped his wife or girlfriend wouldn't detect the *Boadicea the Victorious* perfume.

I strolled nonchalantly through the sliding doors of the hotel and smiled at the young man at the reception desk,

"Yes, thank you, a splendid evening. My host was a perfect gentleman. Oh, is that the time? I really must get some sleep."

Not that there was any need for an alibi. If the police were to investigate the mysterious disappearance of Sir Francis Muir, they would find that Jayne Ryan had disappeared, too. Even an astute investigator would put two and two together and assume they'd gone away together.

In retrospect, what surprised me most about that night was my ability, unlike Lady Macbeth, to go to sleep. I suppose the knowledge of what the Magus intended to do at the solstice took away any sense of guilt: I hadn't murdered him, I'd executed him. Therein lies a very significant difference.

TWENTY-FOUR

CONLEY MANOR HOUSE, WARWICKSHIRE, 19TH DECEMBER 2022 AD

I rang the doorbell of my home and Alice opened it to stare at the sensational auburn-haired woman on her doorstep.

"Can I help you, miss?"

My most captivating smile graced my countenance,

"Yes, you can. You can kiss me."

Alice was outraged and scowled,

"Why would I do that? We've never met...a-and you're a woman!"

I was delighted and enjoying myself. I should have stopped there but, instead, advanced and took her in my arms. How she struggled! She wouldn't let me kiss her and slapped my face. How it reddened and stung!

"Of course, we've met: I'm your husband, silly!"

She went limp in my embrace and pushed me away,

"Jake? B-but that's impossible!"

I laughed and said,

"This is the latest and best of my transformations—I'd rather be a falcon...it's so difficult...what women have to put up with. Are you going to let me in?"

"Yes, but I think you'd better transform back into *my Jake*. You won't get near me, otherwise."

I ran upstairs to the blessed relief of kicking off my tight high heels, unclipping the earrings that also hurt after a while and removing make-up. Alice watched me undress and I heard her gasp in appreciation of my beauty. I concentrated hard and there I was, Jake Conley, naked in my bedroom with my wife smothering me in kisses. Life was much simpler as a man and I sincerely hoped I need never return to being Jayne Ryan.

The morning passed pleasantly as I recounted my adventures to Alice, who, to my relief, considered the elimination of Sir Francis Muir as something obligatory, akin to that of the Führer. She didn't consider me in any way a criminal.

I suppose the illusion of having already saved the planet from an unprecedented catastrophe lasted less than a few hours. First, came a call from Sir Clive Cochrane,

"Good morning, my dear *gell*—"

"Sir, I'm back to being Jake."

"Ah- ah, splendid. You did a splendid job, —er—dear…boy…we need you in a meeting or on video call standby. Can you arrange that?"

I told him I preferred to stay at home and use my tablet on Face Time.

"Excellent! I'll contact you at 3 pm on the dot. You see, removing Frankie was essential, but, unfortunately, not determinant. He was the head of only one Templar chapter. There are several others around the country and they are just as determined to go ahead at the solstice. Need I remind you; it is only three days hence?"

My voice choked,

"So, I killed Sir Francis in vain."

There was a long silence, then,

"Frankie Muir was their inspiration and the most fanatical of the bunch. Consider it as a decapitation. If they are to be defeated, it will be easier with him off the scene. He seemed to have an inexplicable hold over them: practising some kind of mass hypnosis."

"Not impossible to explain. I know how he did it, sir. I'll elaborate on it in my report."

"Good man! However, *Operation Dragon Tail* must go ahead; that is the reason for our meeting. Until 3 o'clock, then...oh, and congratulations on completing a tidy job."

I glared at my mobile. All that suffering as a female and still the operation wasn't complete. In spite of my best efforts, it seemed that a military operation would be necessary to remove the cancerous organisation that threatened our way of life.

The full extent of the danger still hadn't crystallised in my mind until I had an unexpected visit late in the morning. Liffi suddenly appeared in our living room, as if by magic, which it was! The house had once been hers, too. So, I could hardly object when she made herself at home in my favourite armchair. Alice watched on quietly as Liffi said,

"Well, Jake, the time has come. Just three days to the solstice. Nice Christmas tree, by the way."

"Ah, Alice's handiwork, I've just got back from a mission."

"Yes, I know—"

"Do elves know everything?"

"Of course. And I should tell you that your moment has come, Jake Conley. I have known it for many years, ever since I went into a trance in our temple to Freya. It's your wyrd, Jake, but I've come to tell you that you cannot succeed without elfin help."

"I think you need to be more specific, Liffi."

She went on to explain how this situation had happened before in human history and that there was ample iconography, also, and not only, in Christian art testifying to the event. Suddenly, those images made sense.

"You said I'd need elfin help?"

"You will. We will provide you with the weapon, armour and a mount. All three, of course, will be endowed with magic. It means that you should persuade Sir Clive Cochrane to trust you and convince him to call off *Operation Dragon Tail*."

"But won't that mean these masonic Templars getting off scot-free?"

"Jake, compared to preventing the planet from returning to another Ice Age, and in the process saving millions of lives, I hardly think that matters. Most likely, MI5 will round up the ringleaders of the Brotherhood afterwards and charge them with treason. At least, that is what I saw in a vision when I performed the rite of seidhr in Yorkshire, years ago. Jake, it is all woven into your wyrd."

Almost unwilling to accept the inevitable role I had to play, I pressed her for more details. The more she spoke, the more insane the entire affair appeared. To be cast in the role of a saviour on that scale was humbling and beyond my conception. The crazy scheme made me feel ill, but what was the alternative? Ragnarök?

This thought reminded me of an earlier conversation in our days as a couple in the Red Horse Vale.

"Wait a minute, Liffi! Didn't you once tell me we'd face Ragnarök together?"

"I don't know whether this is the famous *end of days* or that scenario is fated for the distant future, but we *will* be facing this side by side, my dear."

With that, she bent over, more beautiful than Jayne Ryan, kissed my forehead, said, "See you at Knoll Down," and vanished.

Alice, who had sat mutely through this encounter, now expressed her opinion.

"It looks like you'd better phone Sir Clive to cancel the military, Jake. The elves know more about human affairs than we do ourselves: and isn't she beautiful? You can trust them."

"It's all right for you to say that—it's not you who has to face the Beast."

I sat back almost in a swoon as I dwelt on what awaited me, I calculated, seventy-nine hours hence. Then, I pondered what Liffi had told me to do and how to achieve it. It seemed fanciful and heroic, but there was one important and comforting detail, it *had* been done before.

Alice's intuition proved as effective as ever. She realised I wouldn't make the fateful phone call until I'd regained my equilibrium. In her mind, this meant bringing me a glass of Lagavulin...and how right she was! As Jayne Ryan, I had enjoyed the finest single malt of my life in Sir Francis Muir's mansion, but when you have a favourite, as I have, it can be a panacea. Brilliant Alice!

Having quaffed a good measure of the restorative amber elixir, I picked up my mobile and tapped the smart key for Sir Clive.

"Dear boy! But it's not 3 o'clock yet."

"I know sir, but something's cropped up."

I went on to explain my visit from the Queen of the Elves and her plan for the solstice.

"Good Lord! Well, I never!"

He was exclaiming about the iconography—it was a revelation for him too.

"It makes a great deal of sense, Conley, but look here, old chap, do you think you're up to this caper? I mean, one man with an antiquated weapon, when you could have the might of the armed forces at your disposal?"

"Of course, I've thought about it a lot, sir. The elves have a vested interest—their world is at risk, too. It's not an antiquated weapon, it's a magic one. The elves are rarely or never wrong and everything makes sense now. The elimination of Sir Francis...at first, it seemed futile, but given the shamanic powers at his disposal, he might well have been able to impede and thwart my endeavours. His removal may well prove fundamental to our success."

"You are a courageous fellow. Bring this off and I'll see you showered with honours."

"Brave? Maybe it was the Lagavulin talking! Whatever the case, the video conference was cancelled and I would be without military support. But this was not a battle to be fought and won using conventional weaponry. The Brotherhood of the Wand was set on an inexorable path of subversion. One man stood between them and the success of their diabolical plan. That man was Jake Conley and whilst I could call on the support of the Light Elves, I knew that the assistance of Freya wasn't available to me. She had foresworn further involvement in human affairs. But I knew that she was my guardian angel...and a seraph, at that! This thought alone gave me strength. I went out to the garage to check my Porsche and turn the engine over. Alice didn't drive it and it had been idle too long. I'd need it to travel down to Avebury on the morning of 21 December.

If everything went well, I'd drive on to London and buy Alice an extravagant Christmas present. Otherwise, there'd be no gift and she'd spend a miserable Yuletide in widowhood.

TWENTY-FIVE
SALISBURY PLAIN, THE WINTER SOLSTICE, 2022 AD

An anxious afternoon and early evening had finally passed. Darkness had descended over Salisbury Plain but the full moon was rising to cast its pale quicksilver glimmer over the landscape. The remarkably few clouds for December must have pleased and suited the proposes of the Brotherhood of the Wand, whose black-cloaked acolytes were already gathered in the henge. I studied them through my night vision binocular. There were at least three hundred of the brethren. I shuddered to think how so many misguided people could share the same perverse vision of a new ice-enveloped world, conceived for the material benefit of an elite.

I wandered over to Knoll Down, my ears alert for any sound that might reveal a betrayal of my presence. I needn't have worried, the only other person there was the silent Liffi, whose voice called gently and sweetly,

"Jake, this way!"

I headed into the trees and found her bathed in moonlight, although she seemed to have her own bright aura, typical of the Light Elves, whenever I saw her. Her corn-coloured hair sheened and she greeted me with a reassuring smile.

"It is beginning, the foe is gathering in the henge to commence satanic rites to reawaken the serpent."

"Hang on a minute! I thought it was a dragon, not a serpent, I'd be fighting."

"Oh, Jake, you who were always the learned one; surely, you remember that the dragon *is* a serpent. You can go right back to the Sumerians and they worshipped Tiamat, the goddess of chaos—"

"That's what Freya said would happen, that the Brotherhood wanted to revive Tiamat to create chaos!"

"There you are, but you will find this serpent-dragon in every culture: the Illuyana of the Hittites, Apep of the Egyptians, Typhon of the Greeks...then those of the Hindus and Buddhists."

"And of course, we have the dragon of the Christian Saint George."

"Yes, but you don't need to fear a fire-breathing beast, that's an invention of the High Middle Ages."

"Oh, thank goodness for that! I'm not going to be roasted tonight!"

She gave one of her tinkling elfin laughs, so pleasant on the ears.

"No, but you will need elfin armour to protect you from the venomous fangs and the iron claws."

"You paint a cheerful picture, milady!"

Again, the adorable burbling laugh,

"Come, there's someone you should meet."

She led me into a clearing and my eyes widened. Talking about shimmering sheen, trotting towards us was a pure white, velvety unicorn. If you'd have asked me five minutes before, I'd have said they were mythical creatures and didn't exist. But of course, on reflection, I'd seen Liffi's alicorn—so, after all, I knew they existed."

"This is my beloved friend, Aerowen, she will be your mount in the fight against the dragon. This is Jake Conley; I have spoken about him with you."

"*Greetings, Jake Conley.*" I heard the voice in my head. "*We must prevail over Jormungand to safeguard our two worlds.*"

I searched my memory, *Jormungand?* Of course, the Norse Dragon that supported Midgard on its back. Hadn't Freya warned me? What were her words? Ah yes, 'The Midgard Serpent, the mythical Jormungand, once aroused will thrash around, rending the veil that separates Midgard from Aelfheim and menacing even the bridge to Asgard...'

'Exactly, Jake, that is what we must prevent.'

"Will I not be too heavy for you Aerowen?"

'Fear not, Master Jake, I am far stronger than I look. And remember, I come from Aelfheim, where we use magic. I can make you seem as but a wren on my back.'

"Jenny Wren? If I can find the pluck of that little birdie, I'll be all right."

Liffi laughed again and Aerowen whinnied,

I looked around and saw that the Queen was holding a mail shirt.

"You must put this on to protect you. Imbued as it is in elfin magic, nothing may penetrate its links."

I shrugged off my parka and pulled the mail shirt over my sweater. It covered me down to the waist and wrists. She handed me a pair of gauntlets and a helm. "There, you look for all the world like Saint George, my dear dragon slayer. Now, mount Aerowen!"

I'd only ever bestridden one horse in my life, so with considerable anxiety I looked at the proud creature. She knew my worries and stepped forward to kneel in front of me. It was easy then to sit astride and when she reared up, I felt secure and well-balanced.

"Now, Jake, take your lance," Liffi pointed to a long, heavy-looking weapon propped against a tree. I wondered whether I would have the strength to wield such a pole. I eyed its bulk apprehensively, but should have had faith. This was elfin manufacture and deceptively lightweight. Liffi passed it to me and I took it up easily, noting the deadly-looking metal head, sharpened to a wicked point.

"Remember, Jake, it's a magical lance and can penetrate even dragon scales, but you should aim to pierce the softer flesh inside the throat and drive the spear into the vital organs."

This sounded easy in theory...but against a dragon!

I tried to be light-hearted,

"Will there be no grateful damsel in distress to be rescued?"

Liffi sounded anything other than jocular, her tone was extremely solemn,

"Naturally, there will be and you'll know her when you see her."

Aerowen trotted to the edge of the trees, whilst feeling like a noble knight errant, I held my lance vertically.

"Wait!" Liffi hissed and we obeyed. With her elfin vision, she had no need for night-binoculars.

"What's going on?"

Liffi shuddered,

"They are conducting their satanic rites, Jake. Can you not hear the diabolical chants? And now as the moonlight strikes the altar stone, they are sacrificing a young girl."

"Is she the damsel in distress?" I was ready to gallop downhill.

"No, there's nothing you can do to save her, Jake, the poor child is doomed. Without her blood, Jormungand will not awaken."

"Curse the fiends!" I cried.

"Jake, succeed this night, and you will be a hero in Aelfheim. I fear on Earth you will not be recognised. The Fate of two worlds, Jake, in your hands. Now go!"

Aerowen cantered down the slope towards the henge but before we were halfway there, the air in front of us vibrated and a great rent appeared. Out of this stepped the White Goddess— the Earth Mother and she cast terrified eyes towards the Black Mass being enacted in the henge.

'There is your damsel in distress!'

I still don't know whether the voice in my head was Aerowen's or Liffi's, but it was clear they were right because as the words reverberated in my brain, the earth beneath the unicorn's hooves quaked and a noise from underground between a rumble and a roar chilled my blood. Out of the ground emerged a serpentine form, first a horned, scaly head with huge fangs then two legs tipped with lethal talons. Had I not seen this; I would never have believed it. The monstrous creature slithered forward towards the anguished, terrified goddess and its maw opened wider, a forked tongue flickering.

"C'mon Aerowen!" I yelled, nudging the poor creature ahead with my knees. She sprang forward, turning around to stand between the monster and the goddess. I lowered my lance, but in that instant the serpent-cum-dragon lunged forward. Fast as it was, Aerowen was nimbler and dodged the serrated fangs ready to poison its victim with deadly venom. I clung to the unicorn's mane with my left hand, and grasped her sides with vice-like knees as she spun around and sprang forward. I saw my opportunity and braced the lance to drive it into the gaping maw. But the dragon was swift, turning its head so that I could see only one yellow eye with its slitted pupil. I seized my chance and buried the needle-like spearhead into the eyeball. With an ear-splitting shriek, the serpent reared, its talons flailing and luckily, not striking us. I needed to press home the advantage and mustering all my force, I rammed the lance deeply through the eye socket and into the creature's brain.

This was not the encounter I had planned. But it was better, more effective. The huge creature rolled over and lay still, the shaft of the lance like a flagpole rising to greet the stars.

'We did it, Jake! Our worlds are saved.' Aerowen's voice caressed my thoughts.

"We did, we did!" I exulted.

I was still trembling from the horrid sight of the evil beast. In the heat of battle, I had not taken in anything of my surroundings. Now, I looked around at the beatific countenance of the White Goddess. She raised her hands to me and I felt a warm and golden glow flow through my body. I knew it was a blessing and meant health. She walked towards us, her face as beautiful as Creation itself. But she stepped past us, smiled, placed a foot on the dragon's head, and its corpse sank beneath the earth, so that the meadow grass sprang up unsullied in vigorous splendour, spangled with unseasonable blooms. The goddess indicated the angled lance planted in the ground. I nodded, nudged Aerowen over to it and pulled it free and used it to salute the deity. As long as I live, I'll never forget her entrancing smile. Behind us, a battle had finished in the henge. Later, I learnt that the Light Elves had slain the wand brethren who had hastened towards the unicorn in an attempt to stop us from destroying the dragon. Among the black-coated bodies, were also those of the evil *døkkálfar*, the Black Elves, evidently having entered the fray on the side of the Brotherhood.

Liffi hurried over, but not in time to greet the White Goddess, who disappeared through a rent between worlds.

"After many centuries, history has repeated itself, my hero! Saint George or, if you prefer, Saint Michael, slew the dragon and now you did the same Jake. The world will be blessed; I expect, with the gift of a bountiful year."

"I think I have already been blessed, Liffi, my body feels so healthy. I might live as long as an elf!"

"That long! I doubt that very much, but you certainly deserve health, wealth and happiness, Jake Conley!"

"What about the bodies?"

"The elves will deal with them. By the way, we saved the girl."

My heart leapt,

"The one on the altar?"

"Yes, she was close to death, but one of ours used elfin magic to save her."

"It's symbolic of this day and it makes me so happy."

"I think you should take off that armour. Aerowen, bear him back to the knoll. I hung your coat from a branch, Jake. Leave the mail shirt and helm there."

"What about you?"

She smiled,

"There's work to be done here. I am their Queen. I give the orders."

"Will I see you again, Liffi?"

I guess I still loved her, but in a different way from my love for Alice.

Was that sorrow on her face?

"You should enjoy your triumph, Saint George! We will meet in the future but not in such happy circumstances. Bless you, my friend."

I swear I saw a tear glistening but it may have been a trick of the moonlight.

In the glade, I changed my armour for my protective parka and looked at the unicorn,

"Aerowen, my thanks and those of all my world for your brave heart."

'I could say the same to you, Jake Conley.'

I stepped over and planted a kiss on her forehead, just below the alicorn. To my consternation, she, the armour and the weapon all vanished in an instant. I was left without a souvenir of my greatest moment, I thought bitterly, and walked down the hill to the site of my victory. I looked in amazement at the wild flowers that had no right to be there in December. Bending down, I plucked six flowers and studied them in my palm. They looked immaculate as if they might never wither and perish. I put them gently into my pocket and hoped that miraculously they never would.

The henge stood forlorn and deserted, as if there had never been three hundred people within its bounds. I wandered over to the altar stone and the moonlight bathed it, but I recoiled because there was still the crimson of the child's blood on its surface. Where would the young girl be? I sincerely hoped that she was experiencing the wonders of Aelfheim after the horrors of Midgard. She was probably some poor orphan, anyway, knowing the warped minds of the so-called Brain Lords. My task now was to report everything to Sir Clive Cochrane and his was to ensure the extirpation of the last of the Templars.

My report would make incredible reading, but I was certain it would finish in the depths of a secret archive. Was there not something more noble about being an unsung hero? I consoled myself that fame, anyway, was a double-edged sword. All told, maybe it was for the best. These were my thoughts as I turned towards the south-west segment of the henge. I stopped suddenly, because a blue light was flickering over the stones and I became aware of an otherworldly presence. Once again, I heard a voice in my cross-wired brain, but this time it was not an elf or a unicorn communicating, but a much more ancient entity.

'Hail, Jake Conley, the blessed! Learn to use the forces of the natural world to promote fertility and healing. Use the gateways to make contact with the spirit. Through the physical world gain access to the spiritual creative life force. Teach your fellow men to connect with their souls and the Earth.'

This indeed, seemed a more worthy goal than any pursuit of illusory fame and fortune. Silence also reigned in my head. I gazed wonderingly at the full moon and the plethora of stars. If I could heed the words of the stones, then my life work would be honourable and fulfilling. I would give it a try, I thought, as I returned to my home and my loving wife. Would she love me more in the New Year, when I became Sir Jake Conley? This was sure to happen. These were my thoughts as I drove through a small village. The pub was still open and swinging from its chains was a painted sign: *The George and Dragon.*

THE END

Dear reader,

We hope you enjoyed reading *The Serpent Wand*. Please take a moment to leave a review in Amazon, even if it's a short one. Your opinion is important to us.

Discover more books by John Broughton at https://www.nextchapter.pub/authors/john-broughton

Want to know when one of our books is free or discounted for Kindle? Join the newsletter at http://eepurl.com/bqqB3H

Best regards,
   John Broughton and the Next Chapter Team

ABOUT THE AUTHOR

John Broughton was born in Cleethorpes Lincolnshire UK in 1948: just one of the post-war baby boom. After attending grammar school and studying to the sound of Bob Dylan he went to Nottingham University and studied Medieval and Modern History (Archaeology subsidiary). The subsidiary course led to one of his greatest academic achievements: tipping the soil content of a wheelbarrow from the summit of a spoil heap on an old lady hobbling past the dig. He did actually many different jobs while living in Radcliffe-on-Trent, Leamington, Glossop, the Scilly Isles, Puglia and Calabria. They include teaching English and History, managing a Day Care Centre, being a Director of a Trade Institute and teaching university students English. He even tried being a fisherman and a flower picker when he was on St. Agnes island, Scilly. He has lived in Calabria since 1992 where he settled into a long-term jobat the University of Calabria teaching English. No doubt his lovely Calabrian wife Maria stopped him being restless. His two kids are grown up now, but he wrote books for them when they were little. Hamish Hamilton and then Thomas Nelson published 6 of these in England in the 1980s. They are now out of print. He's a granddad now and happily the parents wisely named his grandson Dylan. He decided to take up writing again late in his career. When teaching and working as a translator you don't really have time for writing. As soon as he stopped the translation work, he resumed writing in 2014. The fruit of that decision was his first historical novel, *The Purple Thread* followed by *Wyrd of the Wolf*. Both are set in his favourite Anglo-Saxon period.

His third and fourth novels, a two-book set, are *Saints and Sinners* and its sequel *Mixed Blessings* set on the cusp of the eighth century in Mercia and Lindsey. A fifth *Sward and Sword* will be published soon and is about the great Earl Godwine. Creativia Publishing have released *Perfecta Saxonia* and *Ulf's Tale* about King Aethelstan and King Cnut's empire respectively. In May 2019, they published *In the Name of the Mother*, a sequel to *Wyrd of the Wolf*. Creativia/Next Chapter also published *Angenga* a time-travel novel linking the ninth century to the twenty-first. This novel inspired John Broughton's latest venture, a series of six stand-alone novels about psychic investigator Jake Conley, whose retrocognition takes him back to Anglo-Saxon times. Next Chapter Publishing scheduled the first of these, *Elfrid's Hole* for publication at the end of October 2019. The second, is *Red Horse Vale* and the third, *Memory of a Falcon*. The fourth is *The Snape Ring* and is on pre-sale on Amazon. The fifth, *Pinions of Gold* is under consideration by the same publisher. The last of the series *The Serpent Wand* is also under consideration.

The author's next project is to create a 'pure' Anglo-Saxon series.

Lightning Source UK Ltd.
Milton Keynes UK
UKHW011841230920
370426UK00005B/142